IQ High
Crystal Hubbard

© 2013 by Crystal Hubbard

If this book was purchased without a cover, please be aware that it is likely stolen property, reported as unsold and/or destroyed by the publisher, and neither the author nor the publisher received payment for this "stripped" book.

No part of this publication may be reproduced in whole or part, stored in a retrieval system, or transmitted in any form, by any means—mechanical, electronic, photocopied, recorded or otherwise—without the written consent of the author.

For information regarding permissions, please contact Crystal Hubbard at crystalhubbardbooks@yahoo.com

Dedicated to my beloved adopted hometown of Boston, those who suffered in the Boston Marathon bombings of 15 April 2013, and those who ran headlong into the smoke and chaos to do what they could to help the fallen.

All proceeds from the sale of this book will go to the Boston Children's Hospital Emergency and Trauma Fund.

A loud, wet rattle issued from beneath Professor Abernathy's furry white mustache as he hawked into a handkerchief pressed to his pink lips. Sitting at various points around a wide, circular table, the rest of Eichorn High School's four-member Admissions Board winced at the old prof's noisy expectorations. Sean Lindy rose from her seat to pour a glass of cold water from the pitcher in the center of the table. She walked it over to the professor and hovered over him as he gulped down the water.

"Thank you, Ms. Lindy," Prof. Abernathy wheezed. Even though Ms. Lindy had been a newborn the year Prof. Abernathy won his second Nobel Prize in mathematics, she gave him a maternal pat on the back of his worn tweed jacket before returning to her seat.

"Back to business then," said Eichorn Headmaster Sullivan Kennedy. He adjusted the half-glasses perched upon his long nose before glancing down at the profile in his hands. "I'd like to fill the vacancy in the senior class before lunch, if you people don't mind terribly."

"Agreed," said Dr. Nigel Lithgow, head of Eichorn's Music and Visual Arts Department. The portly gentleman swiped a hand through his thinning brown hair. "Let the games begin."

"Marcus Bondoc, seventeen," Prof. Abernathy began, his pale blue eyes squinting at the portfolio of the student he had nominated for admission. "Currently enrolled at Prescott High School in Adler, Missouri, where he carries a 3.98 GPA, Marcus has a recorded I.Q. of 160. He won last year's Nimoy Prize in High School Mathematics and placed second in the national MathMarathon. Marcus was born here in Massachusetts, in Newton. His parents came to the United States from Thailand twenty years ago. His father is a respected neurophysiologist and his mother owns and operates a very successful catering business. The family's average annual income is $390,000.

"Marcus scored 470 out of 500 points on his entrance exam. His math scores were perfect, but he displayed a slight weakness in Spanish and French. In answering the required essay question, Marcus incorporated Newtonian laws of physics and Euclidian geometric theory. Marcus has an aunt, uncle and cousins in Newton, and should he gain admittance to Eichorn, he would reside with them."

A big smile bloomed beneath the professor's wild mustache. "I believe Marcus would make a fine addition to the senior class."

Ms. Lindy studied the boy staring up at her from the photo attached to the Bondoc profile. Marcus looked younger than his seventeen years. He had a wide, bright smile and short, glossy dark hair. Black eyes twinkled against a background of flawless bronze skin. "I agree," Ms. Lindy said. "Marcus would do well here. But he's doing well exactly where he is."

"Dr. Lithgow, who do you have for us this morning?" Mr. Kennedy asked.

Dr. Lithgow's big body shook with excitement. "Cathleen Radcliffe, sixteen. She's a prodigy, a virtuoso on the violin. She has an I.Q. of 150 and she's currently home schooled in conjunction with music instrumentation, composition and theory classes at the Cambridge Conservatory of Music. Cathleen has guested with the royal symphonies of England and Jordan as well as the symphony orchestras of St. Louis, Boston, Chicago, New York City and Philadelphia. At age nine, she played for the president and England's prime minister at the White House.

"Cathleen scored 400 on the entrance exam, with perfect marks on the foreign language segments. Three Ivy League colleges, Julliard and the Sorbonne, are currently pursuing her. Her father teaches music at Carlisle College and Mrs. Radcliffe is a full-time housewife who home schools Cathleen and her three siblings. The family's average annual income is $70,000. Cathleen's guest appearances command upwards of $10,000, all of which goes into a trust until her twenty-first birthday."

"How did she do on the essay question?" Ms. Lindy asked.

Dr. Lithgow withdrew Cathleen's answer from a pile of papers before him. "She quoted the King James Bible and Pindar, and she wrote a concerto." He proudly displayed the chaos of lines and notes etched on the back of Cathleen's essay sheet. "The music is brilliant, and I believe Cathleen would thrive here at Eichorn."

Ms. Lindy squinted at Cathleen's photo and decided that she might have been a pretty girl. It was hard to tell, since Cathleen's head was bowed to one side and her long blonde hair partially cloaked her face. Her shapeless dress had a tiny blue and gold floral print against a beige background that washed out what little color Cathleen had. Her left hand stole Ms. Lindy's attention. It was very small and her fingers were very thin. The pads of her fingertips were thickly calloused, as though she were a lumberjack rather than a violinist. She smiled as she held her violin on her lap, propping it up with her right hand.

"Cathleen doesn't need Eichorn," Ms. Lindy said. "All she needs is that violin."

"Moving on," Mr. Kennedy said, "I'd like to present Linus Merriweather IV, eighteen." He loudly cleared his throat, making sure that he had the attention of Prof. Abernathy, who had a tendency to doze off when talk turned from mathematics to anything else. "Linus is a junior at Hobart & Williams Prep. His I.Q. tested at 140, however he is heir to Merriweather Technologies, one of the world's largest software development companies. The Merriweather family's average annual income is in excess of $3.1 million.

"Linus scored 280 on the entrance exam. He's an avid skier and would have competed for the U.S. in the Winter Olympics had he not suffered an ankle injury while cliff diving in Australia. Linus has a photographic memory. He answered the essay question by referencing the work of Descartes and Milton word for word."

Mr. Kennedy smiled as though the choice for the senior vacancy was now obvious.

Ms. Lindy barely glanced at Linus's photo. His blue eyes, sandy hair and perfect smile were so handsome as to be completely unremarkable. "During his interview with you, Mr. Kennedy, did Linus say why he wanted to come to Eichorn?" she asked.

The headmaster referred to his notes. "Linus stated that Eichorn was the best, and in order for him to become the best, it only made sense for him to enroll at Eichorn."

"I see," Ms. Lindy said. But what she heard was a kid who wanted to come to Eichorn because it was something so many other people wanted. "Did Linus ask you how many applicants had applied for the spot?"

"Why, yes, he did," the headmaster said, curious. "He seemed very interested in that."

"Did you tell him?"

"I gave him my best estimate, about fourteen hundred."

"And how did he react?"

"He seemed ... satisfied." Mr. Kennedy stroked his chin in thought. "Is there some significance to that, Ms. Lindy?"

"None that matters now." She brought her candidate's portfolio to the top of her pile. The sun seemed to shine a little brighter through the tall, wide windows lining one wall of the spacious room. "I'd like to present Charysse DiGregorio," Ms. Lindy said simply.

She watched her colleagues as they perused their copies of Charysse's materials. Mr. Kennedy's eyes continually shifted from Charysse's photo, to her application information and to Ms. Lindy until they finally came to rest, staring at Ms. Lindy over the tops of his glasses. The lines fanning from the corners of his eyes seemed to deepen before he said, "Ms. Lindy, uh, this girl...Charysse..." he began, pronouncing her name as Cuh-REESE.

"It's CARE-iss," Ms. Lindy corrected.

"Very well, then. Charysse." Mr. Kennedy went on. "Her father is deceased and her mother owns a grocery store?"

"That's 'runs' a grocery store," Ms. Lindy said. "Karen DiGregorio is the night manager. She makes $38,000 a year, which makes Charysse eligible for financial aid. You interviewed her. What was she like?"

"Quiet but articulate. Rather personable. She was a lovely girl."

"That's it?" Ms. Lindy demanded.

"What's her I.Q?" squawked Prof. Abernathy.

"She's never been tested," Ms. Lindy said.

"She's enrolled at Lesterville High." Dr. Lithgow's bulbous cheeks reddened in confusion. "That's a public school, isn't it?"

"Yes." Ms. Lindy stood to defend her candidate. "Lesterville's average SAT scores are 360 Math, 240 Verbal."

"Well, she has a 3.8 GPA, but at a school like Lesterville...I'm not sure that's a fair barometer for success at Eichorn."

"It would've been a 4.0 if she hadn't gotten a B in Study Hall."

"Ms. Lindy, I really think you should consider one of the other students we've presented. Miss DiGregorio scored 440 on the entrance exam, and that's respectable, but we have to examine the total picture. Linus submitted a sixteen-page essay, Cathleen gave us twenty pages and a concerto, and Marcus formulated a mathematical theorem to prove his answer. Miss DiGregorio didn't even complete the essay."

"It's right there, on page twenty-eight," Ms. Lindy indicated, displaying the last page of her copy of the profile.

Dr. Lithgow peered at the page. "Three words?"

"The essay question is what we use to determine a prospective student's critical thinking and reasoning skills," Ms. Lindy reminded her colleagues. "The students are told going in that the essay can be the one thing that makes or breaks their application to Eichorn. Of these final candidates, I think Charysse would make the best addition to the senior class. We asked the applicants to answer one question: How many angels can dance on the head of a pin? Read her answer."

Mr. Kennedy's lips moved as he read Charysse's words. Afterward, he pulled off his glasses and touched his palm to his forehead. "Wow," he said, his eyes wide.

"Dear me," the professor muttered, sitting back in awe. "She treated the question as though it were a metaphysical riddle."

Dr. Lithgow gave Cathleen's profile a longing stare before he tossed it over his shoulder, conceding defeat.

"I've already drafted the acceptance letter." Ms. Lindy withdrew it from her slim briefcase. She signed it with a flourish, and then took it to Dr. Lithgow.

"Remarkable, Sean," Dr. Lithgow said, signing off on the letter. "You've done it again."

Ms. Lindy returned to her chair while the headmaster and the professor added their signatures to the letter. She studied Charysse's photo. Judging from the angle of the camera and the size of Charysse's arm in the foreground, she had taken the photo herself with a digital camera and still managed to capture her unique beauty and personality. Deep dimples framed a gorgeous smile that seemed to originate in her wide, coffee-colored eyes. She wore no makeup, but with her toasty brown complexion and long, dark eyelashes, she didn't need it. Her dark hair crackled with auburn highlights and hung in loose waves past her shoulders, and she used her free hand to tuck a lock behind her ear. She wore a light brown sweater that matched her eyes but camouflaged her figure.

Ms. Lindy had never met Charysse, but she already knew a great deal about her. Her exam scores revealed what she knew, her photo showed what she was, and her essay answer – "All of them," – proved her capability.

Ms. Lindy didn't need trust funds, theorems, concertos or I.Q. scores to know that Charysse DiGregorio needed Eichorn ... and that Eichorn needed her.

Chapter One

The room was alive with activity all around her. Spitballs flew from straws pursed between the lips of several boys in low-slung jeans grouped near the windows. Across the room from them, near the door, a group of girls wearing thick eye makeup and chunky gold jewelry huddled over back issues of Spanish *CosmoGirl*. A spitball stuck to the cheek of one of the girls and she whirled around, shrieking profanities in Spanish at the laughing boys. Conversations of students, who were broken into small groups throughout the room, drowned out the teacher's fervent shouts for order.

At a battered desk in the center of the room, Charysse was oblivious to the sound and fury surrounding her. She stared at a white envelope that seemed to float atop the doodles and cuss words that had been carved into the wood-grain printed laminate surface of the desktop. The envelope had come in yesterday's mail, but she still hadn't worked up the nerve to open it. The return address on the envelope had terrified her, and she'd brought the thing to school with her in her backpack. The harder she had tried to forget about the envelope, the easier she thought of nothing else. The envelope had seemed to pulse in her backpack, like a paper telltale heart, plaguing her on the last day of her junior year.

Depending on what the letter said, this would be her last day at Lesterville High. Or, she might be right back in this desk in three months. She would be a senior, unlike a hefty percentage of the kids in the room with her now. A lot of them were being held back, some for the second time. Kurt Almeida, a tall, wiry dark-haired senior who was rolling the mother of all spitballs, was in danger of becoming the first student at Lesterville High who would be old enough to buy his own beer once he actually managed to graduate.

Charysse realized that allowing Kurt into her thoughts was a mistake because now his dangerous attention was on her. It wasn't three o'clock, yet the lower half of his face was covered by a five o'clock shadow that looked like dark sandpaper. Rolling his big spitball between his thumb and forefinger, Kurt sauntered over to her. At twenty, he had the proportions of a grown man, and even the teachers became scenery when Kurt was on the prowl.

He snatched Charysse's envelope from her desk. "Whatcha got here, Encyclopedia Head?"

"Give it back!" she demanded, launching herself at him.

The teacher settled deeper behind his newspaper as Kurt held the envelope out of Charysse's reach with one hand while fastening his other arm tight around her middle. "Oh, Charysse," he moaned, "I knew you'd throw yourself at me one of these days!"

His friends laughed and whistled as Kurt clumsily danced Charysse between two rows of desks. "Is this a love letter? Is it from Mr. Encyclopedia Head?"

Charysse gritted her teeth at Kurt's use of the nickname she most hated. Her entire Lesterville career had been spent being picked on for being "the smart kid." And it wasn't fair. She was no smarter than anyone else. The difference between her grades and everyone else's was that she willing to work for good grades. While she was in her bedroom at night poring over her books, Kurt and his friends were out breaking bottles and throwing rocks at cats in the alley that separated her block from his.

In some ways, she was the most popular girl at Lesterville. She was in all the advanced classes, and everyone always wanted to sit next to her ... so they could cheat off her test papers. The one person who had never teased her or cheated off her was her best friend Bonnie. And it was Bonnie who rescued her from Kurt.

"Thank you very much, Lug Nut," Bonnie said, appearing behind Kurt and plucking the envelope from his hand. She gave the back of his head a sharp smack that made him release Charysse.

"What's your problem?" he complained, rubbing the back of his head.

"You're bothering my girl, that's what." Bonnie's annoyance sharpened her dialect of dropped 'r's and pinched 'a's, a hybrid of Lesterville and her parents' native Cape Verdean. At barely over five feet, Bonnie was almost a foot shorter than Kurt. She seemed taller as she stood there, her red-sneakered feet planted wide apart, staring down Kurt as her jaw fiercely worked over a big piece of bubblegum. "Why don't you go back over to Spitball Central and play with your friends?"

Kurt stared at her for a moment. Beneath a high ponytail of long, curly reddish-brown hair, Bonnie's amber eyes glittered with the fury of a wolverine. She wore an oversized black sweatshirt over black leggings, and with her tiny fists propped on her hips, she looked more than a match for Kurt. Muttering under his breath, he backed away and returned to his friends. They greeted him with sniggering laughter, and Charysse breathed a sigh of gratitude and relief before she sank into her desk.

"You're late," she said to Bonnie.

Bonnie chuckled as she sat backwards in the desk in front of Charysse. "I'm late for a study period." She rolled her eyes toward the teacher. "What's Mr. Creedy gonna do? Write me up? Kurt was molesting you right here in class and he sits up there readin' the stupid Help Wanted ads in the *Globe*."

Bonnie slowly handed Charysse her letter. "So what's this about?" she grinned. "You gonna go to I.Q. High or somethin'?"

Charysse tapped the letter against her empty palm. "I don't know."

Bonnie leaned in closer. "You applied there?" she asked in an animated whisper of shock and horror. "Are you nuts? Eichorn is for like, mad scientists and stuff."

Charysse met Bonnie's concerned gaze. "Remember that science fair I entered in March?"

"Sure," Bonnie shrugged. "You turned pickles into a battery and used it to fire up a bunch of buzzers. That was wicked cool."

"A teacher from Eichorn was one of the judges," Charysse said, smiling at the way Bonnie's "wicked cool" sounded like "wicket cuhl." "She liked my experiment on conductivity, and she told me that I should apply to Eichorn. She said there was one opening in the senior class for next fall."

"Just one?" Bonnie encompassed her classmates in a glance. "Drop-outs and left-backs will open up at least ten spots in our class next year." She glanced at the envelope. "Will it be <u>our</u> class next year?"

"I don't know. I haven't worked up the guts to open it." Charysse ran her fingers over the creamy thickness of the envelope. "It's nice paper. Do you think they'd send bad news wrapped inside such nice paper?"

"Do you really want to go there?"

To her left, Charysse saw the paint peeling from the rusting, criss-crossed security bars bolted to the outside of the windows, a clear indication that they were meant to keep people in rather than out. To her right sat the outdated computer and its cracked monitor, a system that a class of twenty-five students was supposed to share. Under her desk, she ground the heel of her black loafer into a hole that had somehow been gouged into the rubbery cork floor.

Eichorn High, nicknamed I.Q. High, was another world compared to Lesterville. Charysse had seen that immediately when she'd gone there to take the entrance exam. She knew the test would be hard, but she hadn't expected it to be ... well, fun. It had been like a trivia game, but with multiple-choice answers and a page or two of ridiculously hard math problems thrown in. And the essay, that had been the most fun of all. It had almost seemed like a trick question. She had been working on her answer, a lengthy, three-part analysis based on Dante's *Paradiso*, when the simplest, most honest response had come to her like a breath of cool, clean air. The other applicants were still furiously scribbling when Charysse turned in her work and left.

Two weeks later, the headmaster had interviewed her and given her a tour of the school. The six-building campus had once been a teacher's college, and it was situated on sixty-four beautiful acres in Wakefield. The classrooms were airy and carpeted, and there were no holes in the walls. All the computer and lab equipment was up-to-date and intact. Eichorn was also near Wellington University, and many students took classes there.

"Charysse?" Bonnie said, interrupting her reverie. "Do you really want to go to I.Q.?"

"I don't want to say," she answered. "If it's bad news..."

Bonnie grabbed the envelope, tore it open and unfolded the letter.

"It's a federal offense to open someone else's mail," Charysse protested sickly as Bonnie's sharp gaze traveled across the page. "Well? What does it say?" Bonnie, her eyes misty with tears, covered her mouth with her hand as she handed the paper to Charysse.

Her chest tightened and her stomach wrenched into a knot as she softly read her letter aloud. "Dear Miss DiGregorio... We are pleased to offer you a place in Eichorn's incoming senior class..." Her eyes kept tripping over the words, making sure that she was truly seeing what was written and not just what she wanted to see.

"Oh my God, Bonnie!" she finally screamed, capturing the attention of everyone in the room. "I did it! I really did it!" Shivering with excited relief, she threw her arms around Bonnie.

As though weighted with sadness, Bonnie's arms slowly wrapped around Charysse. "Way to go, Encyclopedia Head," she laughed somberly. "What am I gonna do around here next year all by myself?"

Charysse pulled away, holding Bonnie's hands. "This doesn't change anything between us, you know. I'll just be going to a different school, not a different planet."

"Might as well be."

"Think of it this way," Charysse grinned. "Now you'll have *two* schools full of boys to choose from."

Bonnie's sadness evaporated. "I hadn't thought about that. No wonder I.Q. High wants you. You're wicked smart."

Chuckling at Bonnie's compliment, which sounded like "wicket smaht," Charysse began gathering her backpack just as the bell rang. Summer break had finally arrived, and with a loud chorus of cheers, the students fled the room. Mr. Creedy sped out past them in a cloud of newsprint and chalk dust. Bonnie continued to sit on the desk in the empty classroom. "So this is it," she said. "We've been going to school together since I moved to Lesterville in the second grade. This is the end of an era."

Charysse had a hard time thinking of it as an ending when it felt so much like a wonderful beginning. "It's just school." She hung an arm over Bonnie's shoulders. "So we won't be in the same building, big deal. We can still go to Guiglio's after school for those chocolate-covered cannolis you like so much, and we'll have our Brownie Sundae Sundays. It's not the end of anything."

"Maybe not for you," Bonnie murmured as she stood and followed Charysse out of the room.

*

"Do you like the red one or the purple one?" Bonnie held two low-cut, long-sleeved tops up to her shoulders. They were exactly alike, but for the colors.

Charysse, in a preoccupied daze, flipped through the rack of blouses without actually seeing any of them.

"Earth to Charysse," Bonnie said. "We got a fashion issue here."

"I'm sorry," she said with a nervous smile. "What did you say?" She finally noticed the blouses—and Bonnie's impatient expression. "Um…the purple. It goes better with that skirt you bought at Girlz."

"I thought so, too, but I needed another opinion." Bonnie slipped the red shirt back onto the rack. "If you're bored I can finish shopping on my own."

"I'm not bored at all." Charysse adjusted the bags she carried in her left hand to stop their string handles from biting into her palm. "I'm just thinking about Eichorn. And whether I really belong there."

"Here's your proof." Bonnie lifted the two heavy bags filled with the purchases they had made in their trip through the North Shore Mall. "We wouldn't be able to buy any of this stuff if it weren't for you and your big brain. You're ready for Eichorn. The question is, is Eichorn ready for you?" She started for the cashier's stand with an armload of clothes, Charysse quietly following her.

"Is there a uniform at I.Q.?" Bonnie asked when she saw the white button-down shirts and navy and khaki trousers Charysse piled on the counter.

"No. I just want something comfortable that goes with everything."

Bonnie crossed her arms over her chest and rested her weight on her right leg. "You just want to blend in until you're invisible. You want to look like some preppy platehead at I.Q."

"It's Eichorn, and no, I don't." Charysse unrolled a wad of bills and peeled off several twenties to pay for her mountain of clothing. "I just want to be accepted for who I am."

"You're not fooling me, Char. You're crazy scared right now."

"That's ridiculous." Charysse took her change and dropped it into her pocket.

"I know you, Charysse. You've been quiet and jittery for the past week. School starts in two days, and you're so scared I can practically smell it." Bonnie poked her nose in the air and sniffed loudly enough for two other shoppers to turn and stare. "It smells like sweaty gopher feet."

"Okay, I am!" Charysse conceded in a frustrated whisper. "I'm leaving everything I know behind. I don't know any of the kids at Eichorn, or any of the teachers. I won't have my best friend." She pressed her fingers to her lips and Bonnie saw that she had chewed her nails down to the quick. "I think I've made a huge mistake."

Bonnie took her hands. "I want you to promise me something."

"What?"

"Promise me that you won't let them change you." The solemnity in Bonnie's eyes scared Charysse, just a little. "Promise me that you're going to go to I—" She closed her eyes in a long blink. "*Eichorn*—and represent. You show those big brains that someone pretty frickin' special can come from a place like Lesterville, Mass. You're the smartest and nicest person I know, and those kids are lucky to be going to school with you. Not the other way around."

With each of Bonnie's kind words, a layer of anxiety lifted from Charysse's shoulders. She was the lucky one, to have a spitfire like Bonnie on her side. "What do you want to do now?" Charysse asked as she dragged her cumbersome bags toward the exit.

"Let's rent a classic movie and watch it at your place." Bonnie's chocolate brown eyes twinkled. "How 'bout *Mean Girls?*"

"We've seen that a thousand times."

Bonnie laughed. "I just remembered. You're never gonna believe what's on cable tonight. One of the original classics."

"Which one?"

"*Pretty In Pink*! We *so* gotta watch!"

*

Charysse sat in the first desk in the last row of her new homeroom. She had arrived an hour early, so that she could trace her routes from class to class without getting lost. She'd also wanted to be the first one in the room. She felt more comfortable being in class as the other students arrived, rather than walking in once they had all been seated.

Her right knee bounced anxiously as her eyes scanned the room. A wide aisle separated two sets of ten desks divided into two rows of five. The teacher's desk was at the front of the classroom, left of center. Books were neatly stacked on their shelves, sharpened pencils stood tidily arranged in cups and the desktops were so clean, they glowed softly in the fluorescent light. The room had an impersonal cleanliness, as though students never actually used the place.

To help pass the time and calm her nerves, Charysse decided to read the battered paperback she had brought with her. She thought her heart would push through the startlingly white cotton of her shirt when the classroom door swung open at 8:15, and a student walked in. Once her heart rate calmed, she realized that the woman wasn't a student. She looked young, but not as young as a kid. She was slender and moved with the elegant, athletic grace of a dancer. Her black hair was pulled back into a prim bun that made her look only slightly older than she probably was. Her turtleneck, her slim-fitting skirt, her hose and her shoes were all black. Her skin was a pale shade of terra cotta or a dark shade of peach, and it was flawless, but it was impossible for Charysse to determine her ethnicity. She was beautiful in an exotic, James Bond-babe kind of way. Her eyes were her most dynamic feature. They were dark, like ebony, and they shimmered with confidence and intelligence. Once she had you in her gaze, it was hard to look away.

"Hello, Charysse," she said. "I'm Sean Lindy, your homeroom teacher." She offered her hand.

Nerves and fear shriveled Charysse's voice. She was embarrassed by the cool clamminess of her palms as she shook Ms. Lindy's hand. "You got my name."

Ms. Lindy's fine eyebrows met in confusion.

"Most people mispronounce my name," Charysse explained.

"Most people don't take the time to recognize originality. What are you reading?"

"*A Confederacy of Dunces*, by—"

"John Kennedy Toole," Ms. Lindy finished. "That's a wonderful book written by one of literature's greatest lost souls."

A corner of Charysse's mouth hooked into a grin. "An ironic choice, given where I'm sitting right now."

Ms. Lindy gave her tiny smile. "I'm glad you're here, Charysse."

That makes one of us, she thought.

Students began filing into the classroom, some staring openly at Charysse while others appeared completely oblivious to the foreign presence in their midst. As she looked at her new schoolmates, Charysse realized that she shouldn't have put such stock in trading her typical school wardrobe of jeans and T-shirts for the more "scholarly" white shirts and khakis she had bought with Bonnie.

A tall girl breezed by her desk without looking at her. She was very well put together in a red, black and yellow plaid pleated miniskirt, heavy black boots and a tight white button-front shirt. She was thin, and had cat-shaped blue eyes, a Barbie-doll nose and small pink lips set in a permanent pout. With a revealing twirl of her skirt, she set herself prettily at a desk across the aisle from Charysse.

A boy in baggy black jeans and a faded Green Day concert jersey slowed his slouching stride as he neared Charysse's desk.

His short, rust-colored hair looked like it had been finger-combed into soft but unruly spikes. A dimple appeared in his left cheek and his green eyes sparkled as he turned down Charysse's row and sent a piece of paper floating to her on an air current as he passed. Charysse used her hand to pin it to her desk and saw that the paper was covered with what had initially looked like a giant knot of spaghetti. After peering closer, she realized that it was a maze.

The desks quickly filled. Ms. Lindy was closing the door when one more student pushed through it in a jingling flurry of shiny silver bracelets and a strapless top made of some sheer, floaty black fabric. Her candy-apple red lips in a smile and her blue eyes fixed on Charysse, the girl approached her. "Way to go!" she said cheerfully, raising her hand for a high five. Bewildered, Charysse accommodated her, slapping her palm to the friendly stranger's. "I'm Lotus Achearn," the girl said. She stood in front of Charysse's desk, one hand propped lazily on the hip of her oversized, paint-speckled, olive-green cargo pants. "Welcome to Eichorn. Like it so far?"

Charysse smiled nervously. She felt downright dowdy in her soccer mom ensemble while Lotus stood before her with the red straps of her bra showing and her white-blond hair piled in deliberate disarray atop her head. "I've only been here for an hour," Charysse said with a small laugh. "I haven't really formed an opinion yet."

"Very diplomatic, Charysse," Lotus said, pronouncing the name as 'Shuh-reese.'

"Charysse?" Ms. Lindy said, calling her attention as well as stating her name correctly for the benefit of the class.

Hot color sprang to her cheeks at being singled out so early in her Eichorn career. She looked at Ms. Lindy.

"There's a laptop waiting for you in the Student Services office," Ms. Lindy said without looking up from the attendance log on her desk. "You'll need it for your classes today. Why don't you pick that up now, and we can get you registered into the school's network."

"Yes, ma'am." Charysse's color returned to normal. She stood and started away from her desk, nearly tripping over the outstretched shoulder strap of her book satchel.

A brittle laugh pierced the quiet in the room. Charysse turned toward its source – the tall girl in the pleated plaid mini. "Sorry," she said, not sounding the least bit so.

Charysse paused at Ms. Lindy's desk. The teacher's eyes were on the tall girl. Ms. Lindy's expression was blank, although Charysse sensed the annoyance radiating from the teacher's dark eyes. "Ms. Lindy, where exactly is the Student Services Office?" She lowered her voice. "I didn't include that one in my practice run of the campus."

Ms. Lindy smiled, and it was like watching the sun breach the clouds after a heavy storm. "Would one of you escort Charysse to the Student Services Office?"

"I'll do it."

Charysse turned around. Several hands were in the air, but before Ms. Lindy could appoint one of them tour guide, the boy who had given Charysse the maze was already behind her. He bounced his eyebrows.

"The Student Services Office, Marty." Ms. Lindy used her pencil to emphasize her point. "No detours, and don't take the scenic route. First period starts in twenty minutes."

"Yes, sir." Marty saluted briskly. He turned his emerald gaze on Charysse. "Miss DiGregorio?" He grandly gestured toward the door.

"Thank you," Charysse said, leading the way. "I think."

Chapter Two

"Show no fear," Marty advised. Charysse walked beside him as they traveled the length of the long, wide corridor leading to the Administrative Offices. "I'm not scared."

"You should be," Marty chuckled. "Most of us get a little weird when a new kid comes to Eichorn, especially someone like you, but we'll settle once we know your thing."

"My what?" She peeked into the classrooms as she passed them. The classes were fairly small, no more than twenty students in each. But then there were only four hundred students at Eichorn—a third the total of her former class at Lesterville.

"Your thing," Marty repeated, starting down a flight of stairs illuminated by a giant window that spanned two floors. "Your specialty. Norman Webber is the top Math and Computational Speed guy around here. Shane McKenna is the best at Visual Apprehension and Memory. I'm the ace in Spatial and Logic – hence the mazes. Perhaps you've heard of me? Martin Kosh…"

"The A-Mazing Marty," Charysse said with just enough awe to make him smile. "My seventh-grade math teacher told me about you. She gave the class one of your mazes as an assignment once, the one that ran in *Scientia Magazine*." She smiled. "So you're A-Mazing?"

"That's what they tell me," he said with genuine modesty. "If I were to guess, I'd say that you were General Knowledge. You know, you don't sound like you're from Lesterville."

"My mother grew up in Kansas. I guess I adopted more of her midwestern dialect than my dad's Massachusetts. Why did you say that the kids here get weird around new students, 'especially' me?"

"Because one thousand, five hundred and eighty-seven knuckleheads tested for the senior class vacancy and you're the one that got it. You're the one *Ms. Lindy* picked."

Charysse's brow knitted. She didn't understand the significance of the emphasis Marty put on the fact that she had been Ms. Lindy's choice. "How do you know Mrs. Lindy picked me?"

Marty opened the door to the Student Services Office and held it for her. "Norm dug it up." He wiggled his fingers, miming the typing on a computer keyboard. "He gets in everyone's business. How is it that you've never been tested?"

"I've taken lots of tests." Charysse returned the smile of a pleasant-looking secretary as she stepped up to the desk and stated the purpose of her visit.

"Not I.Q.," Marty said, "or else it would have been in your records."

"No one ever asked me to take one."

The secretary took Charysse's Student ID card, and then retreated into another room to retrieve the laptop.

"Maybe you took one without knowing what it was," Marty suggested. "Which would mean that either you're totally off the scales, or…"

"Or?" Charysse prompted.

He smiled. "Or else you're normal."

"I'm normal," she said defensively.

"Pleased to meet you." He took her hand and shook it. "I'm A-Mazing. So are you, and don't you forget it, no matter how hard they try to convince you that you're not."

*

Lunch should have been the easiest part of her day, but with less than two hundred students combined in the junior and senior class, Charysse found that she stood out when she entered the cafeteria. With her lunch tucked in her satchel, she was spared a trip through the long buffet line, but she felt the stares on her as she passed the students lined up for meatloaf, mashed potatoes, grilled chicken breast, peas, garden salad and lemon meringue pie. If Eichorn had nothing else in common with Lesterville, the two schools used the same food service company. As she scanned the room for an empty table, Charysse wondered if Bonnie was in

Lesterville's cafeteria, or if she'd sneaked off campus to eat at Pizzazz Pizza.

"Charysse!"

She tracked the voice to a table in the back of the room, right in front of an emergency exit. Lotus was there, the long, dangling ends of her sleeves dancing on the air as she waved Charysse over.

Clutching the strap of her satchel, Charysse made her way to the table. She was glad to see Marty sitting there, his head down as he etched a design directly onto the table with a fine-tipped pen. There were also two other girls, one of whom looked just like Lotus, only with butter-blond hair and a perfectly average green shirt and blue jeans. Her pale eyes moved rapidly over the pages of a book with no title on its black cover or binding.

"Guys," Lotus said when Charysse had taken an empty seat at the wide circular table, "this is Charysse. She's the new Jamie."

"The new who?" Charysse set her satchel on the floor and drew a piece of paper from it. She slid it to Marty, who looked at it curiously before his face broke in a huge smile.

"When did you finish this?" he asked.

"During second period French," Charysse answered.

"You did it in pen."

"I did it in pencil first."

"It wasn't supposed to have a solution," he said. "It was a trick."

"I figured that out," Charysse said, "right before I would have just chopped the thing in half."

"What the heck are you two talking about?" Lotus asked.

Marty showed them the maze he'd given Charysse.

"It took me two weeks to solve the one Marty gave me on my first day," Lotus said. "He drew a paintbrush, and the maze was this insane scribble of brushstrokes that looked like they'd come from the paintbrush."

"He wrote the word 'plume' over and over to make mine, and I still haven't solved it," said the girl with Lotus's face. "I used it for the cover of my second book of poetry. I'm Chrysanthemum Achearn, by the way. Lotus's older sister."

"*Plume!*" Charysse said, turning excitedly in her chair. "I read your book ages ago! I loved all the poems, but *A Blessing of Unicorns* was my favorite. I loved it because it was a sonnet and not the usual sunshine-and-rainbows ode to unicorns. I wrote a paper on it for my tenth-grade American Literature term paper. I loved how you treated the existence of unicorns as something theoretical instead of mythological."

"Wait a second," Lotus deadpanned. "You actually understood Chrys's poems? Even I don't get her work."

Barely acknowledging Lotus's comment, Charysse set a brown paper bag on the table. "There's a line in the sonnet, 'On silent nights a sorrow overheard'—"

"What's that?" Chrysanthemum blurted, staring in alarm at the paper bag as she scooted back from the table. "If you pull out a peanut butter and jelly sandwich, I swear, I'll just die. I'm not kidding, either."

"I've got grilled peppers and onions on an Italian roll," Charysse told her. "Is that okay?"

"As long as it isn't peanut butter." Chrysanthemum calmed. "Eichorn's nut-free, you know."

"Says you," Marty snorted.

"Nut allergy," Lotus explained, ignoring Marty.

"Or just plain nutty," Marty muttered.

"She freaks whenever someone shows up with a brown bag," Lotus said. "I'm the alpha twin. The dominant, extroverted, laidback, *normal* one."

"I'm the beta," Chrysanthemum said. "The submissive, antisocial, introverted, high-strung, *older* one. By seven minutes."

"You and the seven minutes," Lotus grumbled. She turned her attention back to Charysse, who was staring at a group of children sitting at another table. The kids were laughing and pitching bits of food at each other. Most of them looked like fourth graders, a couple of them so short their feet didn't touch the floor.

"Does this school have an on-site day care for the teachers?" Charysse asked.

Marty laughed. "No. Those are Corcoran snot wipes. They take math and science classes here."

Charysse slightly shook her head, once again embarrassed by her ignorance of all things related to Eichorn.

"Corcoran is the gifted elementary school that feeds Busch, the gifted junior high that feeds Eichorn," Lotus said. "Most of the kids here at Eichorn have gone to school together since kindergarten."

"The Natives," Marty said ominously, his face still on his work.

"Chrys and I came here as sophomores. Candice came last year."

"Hi," said the remaining girl at the table. She sat hunched over, pressing the pad of her forefinger to her plate to catch the last crumbs of her lemon meringue pie. Her brown hair hung lankly, almost touching the sticky remains. Her brown eyes were small and set deep in her face, giving her a haunted appearance that made Charysse instinctively want to put an arm around her thin shoulders. Her T-shirt was the same flat brown as her hair and eyes, and with her beige skin, she seemed to vanish in the presence of her more colorful tablemates.

"The Natives are lifers," Lotus said. "They've been in the gifted system since they were fetuses." She pointed to various faces around the room. "Arija Benjamin is a Native. Remember her? She's in Homeroom with us. So's Mackenzie Cole."

Charysse followed Lotus's gaze and saw Mackenzie, the tall girl in the pleated plaid skirt, sitting at a table. The wide, round tables accommodated eight, but there were only two other girls sitting with Mackenzie. They leaned over her elbows as she flipped through the pages of a bridal magazine.

"Interesting lunch reading," Charysse remarked before turning back to her sandwich, which Marty eyed hungrily.

"She's probably picking out the dress she wants to wear when she marries Shane," Lotus said with scornful snicker.

"Who's Shane?" Charysse passed Marty half of her sandwich before starting on the remaining half. He shoved aside his untouched tray of cafeteria meatloaf and took a huge bite of the sandwich.

"Shane McKenna." The name left Lotus's lips like the notes of a song. She dreamily stared at nothing as she used her straw to slowly stir the ice melting in her cola. "He spends lunch hour at Wellington University. He takes math there."

"Are they one of those couples that met in the kindergarten sandbox and have been together ever since?" Charysse smacked Marty's hand when he reached for one of her homemade butterscotch brownies.

"Shane and Mackenzie?" Lotus asked.

Charysse nodded. She split each of her brownies in half, offering a portion to each of her tablemates.

"Only in Mackenzie's mind," Chrysanthemum laughed as she took a piece of brownie.

"Big Mac isn't Shane's type," Marty said, his cheek bulging with brownie. "She's like a pedigreed French poodle – pampered, spoiled, and one of the most vicious animals in nature."

"If the Wicked Witch of the West and Lord Voldemort had a baby, it would be Mackenzie Cole," Chrysanthemum said from the pages of her book. "She called dibs on Shane their first day of nursery school."

Lotus leaned closer to Charysse. "Personality aside, she can have any guy in this school," she whispered.

Marty kept his gaze on Charysse. "Not me."

" 'Venus, thy eternal sway, all the race of men obey,'" Chrysanthemum muttered, her attention to her book never wavering.

"Whose is that?" Lotus asked.

"Euripides," Charysse said in concert with Chrysanthemum, who smiled, but still didn't look up.

"What does it mean?" Marty asked.

"Boys are stupid," Chrysanthemum answered.

"You have to admit that Mackenzie is pretty," Charysse said.

Lotus wrinkled her nose. "I guess..."

"Not on the inside," Marty said.

"I don't want to waste my lunch hour talking about Big Mac." Lotus crossed her arms on the table. "Let's talk about you, Charysse. What do you like to do for fun?"

"The usual stuff, I guess. I like to play trivia games."

"Oh." Lotus's smile faded a bit. "That's ... nice."

"At bars. For money."

Everyone at the table perked up, even Candice.

"My friend Bonnie and I make the circuit with her brother. He's twenty-two, so we get in with him. He's our cover."

"I really like the sound of this," Lotus said. "Tell me more."

"There's this bar in the Back Bay, near the State House. There's mostly lawyers and government workers in there when we go. Wednesday night is Trivia Night, and the winnings can get up into the hundreds. They play ten games. You have to get a perfect score to win, and if no one wins, that game's pot rolls over to the next game."

"How much can you win?" Lotus asked.

"I won enough this summer to pay for my books, my lab fees and a new wardrobe."

"Your mom lets you hang out at bars?" Candice's voice, like a quiet wind rustling between trees, barely reached them from across the table.

"She works nights, from four to midnight." A wan smile came to Charysse's face. "I haven't seen her in five years, when she started taking the second shift."

"What do you think?" Lotus said, exchanging a look with Marty.

"I think we've found our tenth," he said, his eyes fixed on his drawing on the table.

"Tenth...?" Charysse wondered aloud.

"You're the tenth Transfer," Chrysanthemum explained. "Lotus and I came in tenth grade with Donovan Rainey. Marty came in freshman year with Crandall Fried, Lynn Michaels and Zachary Levine. Candice transferred in last year with Luke Miller, and this year, you came in solo. We Transfers didn't play in the Corcoran or Busch Leagues. We're the strangers in a strange land."

Marty lifted his orange juice carton in a toast. "Here's to the tenth Transfer."

The girls raised their beverages.

"What happened to the kid I replaced?" Charysse asked.

"Jamie Rivers," Candice said wistfully.

"You know that fine line between madness and genius?" Marty said. "For Jamie, it was like a rubber band. And it snapped."

"Jamie was big-time General Knowledge and Math," Lotus said. "By the time he was ten, he'd been on all the talk shows and had papers written about him. He could have gone to college at fourteen, if his parents had been able to make him."

"Jamie refused to go," Chrysanthemum said. "So they sent him here."

"Jamie's a good guy, but he never wanted to be at Eichorn," Marty said. "He never wanted the talk shows or the magazines or any of it. He just wanted to be a regular person."

"Or less of a show pony," Chrysanthemum said.

"So in January he comes back from Winter Break and starts acting really crazy," Marty said. "He's picking food out of the garbage cans, he's going to class every day in the same clothes he's worn for a week."

"He almost gave Mrs. Kinmount a coronary when he walked into Physiology with a shaved head and wearing a frilly pink sundress," Lotus said.

"The school put up with it for a while," Marty continued. "There's always some kid trying to Section 8 out of this place. But then Jamie stopped speaking. He didn't talk to anyone, ever. They sent him to shrinks and therapists, even a hypnotist, but nothing worked. His parents took him out of Eichorn over Spring break and sent him to some school in Switzerland."

"That's so sad," Charysse said.

"No, it isn't," Marty chuckled. "That's the thing. Jamie's at a boarding school, but he says other than that, it's just a regular school. He can even take Skiing as a Phys. Ed. course if he wants to. There was nothing wrong with Jamie, except that he wanted to get the heck outta Eichorn. He wanted to have a normal life. He faked the whole crazy."

"Lucky guy," Candice mumbled.

"You're scaring me," Charysse said. "Is Eichorn really that terrible?"

"The school is great," Lotus said. "It's the Natives you have to watch out for."

*

The last hour of the day brought Charysse back to Ms. Lindy's room for a class with the unrevealing title of *Lindy: 401*. She took the seat she had claimed during homeroom and opened her laptop. Even though she had used the computer in all of her classes, she still hadn't created her own school e-mail account, so she set about doing that as her classmates trickled into the room. The school system kept logging her off, and after her long first day, she was starting to get annoyed.

She flinched when an arm reached from behind her and keyed in a series of letters and numbers. "You have to log onto the school's network with the universal password, then create your account with your own password."

Charysse turned in her seat to say thanks, but the words stuck to her tongue as she stared into the face of Heaven on Earth. His eyes were the storm-tossed blue-green of a New England summer sky, and his skin seemed to glow with the vestiges of his deep summer tan. Straight white teeth peeked at her through his unassuming smile. Charysse's breath locked in her chest when he passed his hand through the thick locks of his wavy dark hair.

"I'm Shane McKenna," he said. "You're Charysse?"

She detected a slight trace of an accent – English, Irish, possibly even Australian – but she couldn't label it for certain. His surname was Scottish, so maybe that's what it was. She took the hand he offered, but still couldn't take her eyes off his. "You said it right," she finally managed.

His dark eyebrows almost met in an expression of curiosity.

"Most people say 'Sha-REESE,'" she explained. "You said 'CARE-iss.' You said my name correctly. Thank you."

"No problem," he smiled. "Congratulations on making it through your first day."

She laughed. "It could have been better."

"Let me guess..." He thoughtfully stroked his chin, drawing her gaze to the wonderful shape of his mouth. "Professor Abernathy called you to the board in Advanced Calculus. You got the right answer, but since you didn't solve the problem his way, he chewed you up in front of the class. He only does that to the students he likes, so don't take it personally. French was better. Madame Frazier complemented your fluency and comprehension, but you got stuck sitting in the desk right in front of her podium." Shane leaned forward. Charysse's heart responded with a thump so hard she thought he would hear it. "It could have been worse. She spits so much in her German class, the kids in the front row have to wear wetsuits."

Charysse bit back a laugh.

"You were late for Art History, but Miss Lockhart is pretty lax about punctuality, so you were able to relax enough to whisper to Lotus through the whole class."

"How is it that you know so much about me and my day?"

"I know about your day because I was there, for a lot of it. I don't know anything about you, other than that you were so nervous today, you didn't notice me in any of the classes we had together. Including this one."

"What is this class anyway? I didn't register for it."

"I think all of us were assigned here. As for what it is, I don't know."

"That's the first time today I've heard those three words."

"Since you brought up the subject of three words, your entrance essay has become an Eichorn legend."

"How do you know about that?"

He flashed his knee-melting smile once more, and Charysse felt as though her head were suddenly filled with helium. "Haven't you heard? Eichorn kids know everything."

Ms. Lindy entered the room with Mackenzie Cole shadowing her. Conversation ceased as Ms. Lindy went to her desk. Mackenzie, her books clutched against her chest, stared at Charysse as she found an unoccupied seat. Ms. Lindy's voice broke the tense visual contact between the two girls. "As you were," the teacher directed, as if she expected students to talk and visit during her class.

A tall thin boy dressed in a black, short-sleeved button-down and black slacks vaulted to his feet. He bounced from foot to foot and kept putting one hand on his hip while the other constantly adjusted the thick, black-framed Dexter propped crookedly on his face. "Ms. Lindy, exactly what class is this?"

Charysse stared wide-eyed at the boy's demanding tone and perpetual fidgeting. Any teacher at Lesterville, even the cowardly Mr. Creedy, would have put him out of class for speaking out that way. But Ms. Lindy calmly looked up from her work and set down her pen before she answered. "You didn't find a syllabus when you hacked into my files, Mr. Webber?"

"I'm just wondering what this class is about, that's all," Mr. Webber said defensively. "What are you supposed to *teach* us?"

"Have you ever considered loosening that stranglehold you have on regimentation, Mr. Webber?" Ms. Lindy said.

"Yeah, Norm," Marty piped from the back of the class. "You seem to have twisted your screws a little tighter over the summer."

Charysse watched Norm Webber in amazement. The kid screamed raw nerve. From the tips of his crudely chopped black hair and the permanent flush in his pale cheeks to the scuffed toes of his black sneakers, he was a scratching, squirming, twitching, hitching, rubbing, wiggling, bouncing, jiggling, jittering stick figure.

"What do *you* think this class is about, Mr. Webber?" Ms. Lindy asked.

Her answer seemed to elevate Norm's anxiety level, and he began to shiver. "So it's Socratic Method time, huh? Answering my questions with questions so I can figure this class out on my own?"

Ms. Lindy smiled slyly. "So have you figured it out yet?"

Norm dropped back into his desk, grabbed his head and began to rock back and forth. He mumbled to himself as he flipped open his laptop and logged onto the Internet. It seemed to sedate him as he watched his screen, and Charysse was close enough to him to see the reflection of it in his glasses. He was looking at math problems. Chaos math problems.

"Any more questions?" Mrs. Lindy asked brightly.

Mackenzie gracefully poked a slender arm into the air and prettily wiggled her fingers.

Ms. Lindy briefly met Charysse's eyes before she addressed Mackenzie. "Yes. Miss Cole."

"What—" she began, looking at Charysse, "sorry. I meant, *who* is that?"

Charysse turned to see Mackenzie's finger pointing at her.

"Charysse, would you stand please?" Ms. Lindy said. Charysse did so, straightening the front of her khakis. "Class, I want each of you to tell Charysse your name and something about yourselves." She gave Norm a pointed look. "Something that won't give her nightmares."

Charysse had already met Marty, Lotus, Candice and some of the other students from homeroom and other classes. She had experienced enough Norm, so she wasn't offended when he looked at her, turned blood red, and muttered, "I'm busy," before pushing up his glasses and burying his face deeper in his laptop.

She hadn't met the first boy who spoke. He had long, maple-brown hair and pretty cinnamon eyes, the wild, poetic good looks of a rock star. As he spoke, he toyed with the tiny peace symbol hanging from a leather cord around his neck. "I'm Donovan Rainey," he said. "And I'm from Scarbury."

Charysse responded with a tiny smile of surprise. Scarbury and Lesterville were neighboring towns.

Bradley Hogan was another new face. "I'm Brad," he said as he stood. "I'm sixteen, and if you ever need help with Organic Chem., I'm your man."

Charysse nodded gratefully. She didn't know about his chemistry talents, but she had doubts about his claim to manhood. He was all of five-foot-nothing and probably weighed as much as her right leg. His bright red hair was thick and cut in a blunted style that made him look like a pixie. When he smiled, his lips disappeared to expose a mouthful of metal.

Charysse wasn't terribly surprised when Mackenzie stood and approached her for an introduction. "Mackenzie Cole," she said, her unblinking stare fixed on Charysse. "I've heard about you." She offered her hand, fingers down, as though she were the Empress Josephine. Charysse took her thumb, gave it a friendly shake, then stuck her hands in her pockets. Mackenzie continued to stand there, leaning one hand on Shane's desk.

Charysse had no interest in playing games. Mackenzie's statement was designed to make her uncomfortable, to make her seek information that only Mackenzie had. So Charysse flipped it. "I've heard a lot about you, too, but I'm sure most of it was exaggeration."

Mackenzie's icy smile melted into a fierce pout. She turned and went back to her desk, but not before Charysse saw her tightly clenched fists.

Shane stood next. He reached forward, took her hand and gave it a firm but gentle shake. "I'm Shane McKenna, but you know that already. And ... I'm glad you came to Eichorn."

A blush climbed from Charysse's shirt collar and didn't stop until it warmed her scalp. She sat down to hide her face from the class. And Shane.

"Thank you, class," Ms. Lindy said. "I have some work to do, so I'm sure I can trust you people to find constructive ways to occupy this hour."

The students looked lost and then amused as they rotated their desks or left their seats entirely to converse with their friends. Charysse spent a moment watching Ms. Lindy. The teacher worked at her desk, but she seemed to spend more time looking at the students than the leather-bound notebook opened in front of her.

She's watching us, Charysse thought.

"Are you busy after school?" Shane asked her, stealing her focus from Ms. Lindy.

"I'm meeting someone. My friend Bonnie," she added hastily. "We made plans to get cannolis after school. She likes the chocolate-dipped ones, but I like the plain ones better. Bonnie's still at Lesterville and..." She waved her hand, putting an end to what must have been boring babble to him.

"It's good to have friends on the outside. Are you free tomorrow afternoon?"

Before she could say no, Mackenzie appeared, looming over them with her arms crossed over her chest. "Shane, I was wondering if you'd like to join us over there." She threw her head toward the circle of desks near hers. "We're just talking about what we did over the summer. You know...catching up." She stabbed a sharp glance at Charysse. "You can come, too."

"Thanks, Mac, but I'm good," Shane said.

Curiosity won out over common sense, and Charysse started pushing her desk to the circle.

"Great," Mackenzie said with mock enthusiasm before returning to her seat.

Shane sighed. "As goes your nation, so goes mine." He pushed his desk over, too.

Donovan and Bradley flanked Mackenzie, and several other students filled out the circle with Shane and Charysse. Marty had moved to the long, wide windowsill, where he worked on a maze in a notebook opened across his knees. Candice sat in her desk in the corner, reading, partially hidden by the shadow of a bookcase. Norm was still glued to his happy and peaceful world of calculations and hypotheticals.

"We're playing a little game," Mackenzie said. "Let's call it...I Know What You Did—Or *Didn't*—Do This Summer." She fixed her cat-like stare on Shane. "If your summer were a horror movie, would you live or die?"

"I'd die," Marty called from the window, "but only to get away from you."

"What about you, Candice?" Mackenzie directed toward the corner, her voice heavy with condescension.

"I'd live. Or maybe I'd die. I'm not sure," Candice said. Bradley and Mackenzie snickered, which sent Candice slumping lower in her seat.

"I'd live," Bradley said, his sudden blush swallowing his freckles. "Unfortunately."

"I'd die." Donovan yawned coolly. "A few times, actually."

It was Shane's turn. He sat back in his chair, one arm hanging over the back of it as he absently doodled in a notebook. He didn't look up as he said, "I would languish on life support, but then I'd make a miraculous recovery."

Donovan, Bradley and Marty applauded, but the boys quieted when Mackenzie said, "It's your turn, Charysse. Would you live or die?"

"What about you?" Charysse countered. "You never said."

"I would live," she said airily.

"So would I."

Mackenzie's eyes narrowed as her upper lip pulled into a slight sneer. "So you're a virgin?"

Several heads whipped around to see if Ms. Lindy had overheard Mackenzie's audacious question, but the teacher seemed to be absorbed with whatever she was writing in her ledger.

"So we're not speaking in movie code anymore?" Charysse countered.

"I'm surprised, that's all," Mackenzie said.

Charysse arched an eyebrow.

"Oh, come on," Mackenzie laughed. "You're from *Lesterville*. Don't you all get married and start having babies by Junior Prom?"

Marty hopped off of the windowsill. "Is that all you got, Mac? With your superior Intuition, that's the best insult you can come up with? You must have forgotten to take your Nasty Pill this morning."

"Who asked you, Maze Head?" Mackenzie snapped, slamming her palms on her desktop as she stood. "You tried to seduce the new girl with one of your Rainman squiggleworks, and now you're her knight in faded denim? You want me to take a good look at her? Fine, I will." Mackenzie rounded her desk and leaned back on the front of it, her incisive glare traveling over Charysse. "You're a good girl and respected, and you're probably here at Eichorn on the recommendation of a teacher. You're confident and independent, but you didn't have the guts to have pursued Eichorn on your own, and you never would have, if you'd known how tough the competition for the spot would be." She glanced at her classmates. "Ignorance gave the smart kid confidence."

Even though Charysse kept her eyes on Mackenzie, she noticed movement from Ms. Lindy's desk in her peripheral vision.

"You're working class, but not low class, and you're not fooling me with the Young Republican wardrobe. But it's the first day of school and I suppose you wanted to make an impression. You're wearing no jewelry and no makeup, so what we see is exactly what we get. There's an air of sadness about you, or maybe it's maturity. Either way, it makes me think that something happened to force you to grow up a little faster." Her gaze flickered downward, to Charysse's hands. "And you don't have any anxieties I can see, at least not right now." Her eyes glittered. "But I'll find them. I always do." Mackenzie took a deep breath before continuing. "You were probably the brightest student at that dump of a school in Lesterville. Your entrance exam essay showed that you've got just enough cunning to fool people who should know better into believing that you're Eichorn material. You talks to boys as friends rather than potential love interests, so I doubt that you've ever had a serious relationship."

"I'm not a flirt, if that's what you mean," Charysse said crossly, suddenly reaching the limit of her patience. "Have you ever turned that genius intuition on yourself, Mackenzie? I wonder if you see what I do, a pretty girl who slathers on makeup because she doesn't want people to see her real face. I see someone who wears high heels because it's the only way she can get people to look up to her." The longer Charysse stared at Mackenzie, and the angrier she became at being singled out, the more clearly she saw this young woman's true nature. "I see someone who takes pleasure in belittling others to make herself feel more important. I'm looking at a person who attacks when she feels threatened, even when no threat exists. I see a girl who's losing control."

Mackenzie's pursed lips turned white. "Intuition," she said stiffly. "I guess I missed that."

"That's not the only thing you should know about me, Mackenzie." Charysse pulled her desk back into its original position. She grabbed her laptop and shoved it into her book satchel. There were only five minutes left to the period, so she put on her jacket. "Ms. Lindy," she said, "may I please be excused?"

Shane went to Charysse. "Don't let Mac get under your skin. The rest of us just ignore her. You'd be surprised at how well that actually works."

"I'm tired and I want to go home," she said softly without meeting Shane's gaze. "Mrs. Lindy, may I?"

"By all means," the teacher said.

Charysse was crossing the threshold when Mackenzie impatiently called after her. "Well, what's the other thing I should know about you?" she demanded.

Charysse didn't turn around. She didn't want Mackenzie to see her satisfied smile. "I'm 'wicket smaht,'" she answered in her best Lesterville accent.

*

"I waited for you at Guiglio's for thirty-five minutes," Bonnie greeted from the top step of Charysse's front porch. It was almost seven o'clock and Charysse was so tired, she dragged her book satchel behind her as she climbed the stairs to her darkened triple-decker home.

"I'm sorry. I got off the T at the wrong stop and ended up trapped in Woburn. I'm going to have to get a car and start driving myself to school."

"Tough day at the office, pal?" Bonnie nudged her with an elbow and handed her a cannoli, heavily dusted in powdered sugar and bundled in white bakery paper.

"You wouldn't believe some of the kids there," Charysse said around a hearty bite of the rich dessert. She licked her fingers. "There's this one kid, Norman Webber. He's like a squirrel on crack. Seriously. And there's this girl, Candice. It's like she was replaced by her own shadow. Remember in seventh grade, when Mrs. Hampton handed out that insane maze for us to do for extra credit? And she made us read that newspaper article about the kid who drew it?"

"'The A-Mazing Marty,'" Bonnie said with a comical wag of her head, her words forming white wisps in the cool night air. "I never did figure out that maze, and I got so sick of hearing about that kid. Talk about A-nnoying."

"He goes to Eichorn. He's in my homeroom and my Lindy class."

"What's a Lindy class?"

"No one knows. It's weird. We just sit there and do whatever and she watches us."

"Like Curious Creatures," Bonnie giggled. "Remember that birthday party we went to in the fourth grade, the one where they had the snakes and skunks and toucans just wandering around?"

"Well, it wasn't quite like that." Charysse licked a bit of filling from the palm of her hand. "Actually, it sort of was. I don't know what Ms. Lindy's up to. She's definitely not like any teacher I've ever had." She opened her satchel, withdrew the maze Marty had given her, and showed it to Bonnie. "It looks like the Gordian knot. Wild, huh?"

"What's Gordon's Knot?"

Overlooking Bonnie's mispronunciation, Charysse explained. "It's a knot that was so complicated and so hard to untie, that the only one supposedly able to do it was the person meant to rule Asia. Alexander the Great couldn't untie it, so he just cut it in half with a sword."

"That's what I would have done," Bonnie said. "So basically what you're sayin' is that Eichorn is full of freaks and geeks?"

Charysse flinched, a little hurt by the unintended insult. "I guess. The school has a lot of money," she said, changing the subject somewhat. "A lot of the kids have patents and copyrights for their inventions and publications and stuff. The school keeps a small percentage of the rights, and with the money it earns, it funds scholarships, the libraries and special programs. There's one kid in my class, Crandall Fried, who invents food products. Last year he patented a process to cross chicken with turkey. It's called 'Chirkey,' and he calls it the 'Biggest Breasted Bird.' Apparently it's a real hot ticket in Japan. There's a kid in the junior class who's researching genetic memory. He's been breeding mice since he was in the ninth grade. He taught the great-great-granddaddy mice to run a maze to get food, and the latest generation seems to know the maze without having been taught. There's another guy who invented moist toilet paper that has the texture of the human tongue, and—"

"So you like it there?" Bonnie interrupted, shivering within her denim jacket.

Not wanting to hurt her, Charysse understated her feelings. "It's okay."

"What are the boys like?" Bonnie asked gleefully.

"One guy seemed pretty normal," Charysse grinned.

"Saving the best for last! What's his name?"

"Shane McKenna."

"Sounds good so far. Does he talk backwards or have the Periodic Table tattooed on his butt?"

"He has the nicest voice." Charysse slumped dreamily against Bonnie.

"Is that your way of saying he has a big, shiny forehead and thick Poindexter glasses?"

"No. He's not bad looking at all." Charysse knew that she couldn't find the right words to properly describe the way Shane's voice in her ear had made her skin tingle. Even if she could, she knew that Bonnie wouldn't place a boy's voice among his most interesting features.

"Jeez, Char, that's the best you can say about him?"

"He's also really nice. He wanted to know if I was busy after school tomorrow."

"And?"

"I never answered. A girl named Mackenzie totally went off on me. She's a real head case. No lie." Bonnie listened intently as Charysse gave her the play-by-play of her interactions with Mackenzie.

"You want I should pick you up from school tomorrow and job her in the parking lot?" Bonnie offered.

"Thanks, but no. I gave it right back to her. She'll probably leave me alone from now on."

Bonnie raised a skeptical eyebrow. "I'm not the genius on this stoop, but I've seen enough *Animal Planet* to know that Little Miss Mackenzie is not gonna back down. You've angered the queen bee, Char. She's gonna want control of the hive, and there's only one way for her to get it."

Charysse swallowed nervously. "You think she's going to kill me?"

Bonnie shrugged. "Not for real. But she can definitely make life miserable for you. You're on her turf, after all."

But it's my turf now, too, Charysse thought. As she said goodnight to Bonnie and watched her get into her car, she felt even more anxious now, at the end of her first day, than she had at the beginning.

Chapter Three

"**M**iss DiGregorio, is my lecture on Pavlovian response boring you?" Dr. Theodore Lemke asked, pinpointing his attention on Charysse.

"No, sir," she answered. "I was just wondering why you have a bag of money on the top of your bookcase."

There were twelve students in Dr. Lemke's Behavioral Science class, and Charysse sat in stunned silence as each of her classmates groaned, clapped or whistled. Even Dr. Lemke's craggy face collapsed into a broad, cartoonish grin. "You've been coming to this room for almost two months now, and finally, you've asked about Lemke's Treasure," Dr. Lemke said. "My dear, I admire not only your curiosity, but also your healthy respect for my lectures. Most of my new students are so bored by my class that their minds wander within ten minutes of my first lecture, and I find them immediately asking about that 'bag of money.'"

Charysse guiltily bit the inside of her lip. She'd noticed the bag of money upon entering the classroom on her first day in September. As the semester had progressed, she'd wondered not so much why the money was there, but why it hadn't been stolen. It wouldn't have lasted a day at Lesterville.

The teacher stepped toward the bookcase. The flaps of his wool jacket stirred up clouds of dust from the stacks of psychology texts and journals stacked haphazardly about his cluttered, windowless classroom.

"Who would like to explain Lemke's Treasure to Miss DiGregorio?" he asked.

"It's a problem-solving thing," Bradley offered.

"It's more than a 'thing,' boy!" Dr. Lemke boomed. Grunting from the effort, he stood on the bottom shelf and stretched his left arm to grab the treasure with the very tips of his fingers. "It's a challenge!" He tossed the bag, and it landed with a soft thump on Charysse's desk. The accompanying cloud of dust made her sneeze.

"Lemke's Treasure is supposed to illustrate man's ability to adapt and problem solve," explained Shane, who sat next to Charysse in the small, circular arrangement of desks. The whole class watched him pick up the bag. "There's something in here that each of us would love to have. The challenge is how to get to it, without breaking any of Dr. Lemke's rules."

Dr. Lemke stood before Charysse, his hands clasped at his lower back. "Are you up to the challenge, Miss DiGregorio?"

"It depends. How much is in the bag?"

The room went dramatically quiet as Dr. Lemke said, "Six hundred dollars, American."

"No way," Lotus gasped, her pale eyes wide and her orange-glossed lips in an astonished "o."

"Yes. Way," Dr. Lemke said. "With each year that passes in which no student rises to the challenge, I add five more Andrew Jacksons to the bag. No student has managed to conquer the challenge of Lemke's Treasure since its inception."

"What are the rules?" Charysse asked.

"You must take the money from the bag," Dr. Lemke began, "without harming in any way the money or the components of the bag. The one who opens the treasure may claim it for his—or her—own."

Charysse studied the bag for a moment. It appeared to be a simple pouch made of a circle of clear plastic. The bag had been gathered around the money and tied at the neck with a length of ordinary household twine. "That's all?" Charysse asked. "Is this a trick?"

The class laughed openly while Dr. Lemke only shook his head and chuckled. "My dear, Miss DiGregorio, you've proven yourself to be a thorough and thoughtful addition to my class, however some of my very best students have been confounded by Lemke's Treasure. It's no trick, although I myself have no idea how to open the bag. Each year I have to tear open the old one and put the money in a new one."

"Nobody likes free money more than I do, Charysse, but even I couldn't figure out how to get that bag open," Bradley said. "I tried to steam the twine, to loosen it enough to untie the knot, but all it did was gunk up the plastic. It tore the second I tried to untie the knot."

"I oiled the twine," Lotus said. "The plastic stayed intact, but I still couldn't work out the knot."

"Everyone in school has tried it," Shane said. "No one's been able to get that money."

Charysse, her brow wrinkled in disbelief, glanced at her classmates and then back at the bag. "You're kidding, right?"

Dr. Lemke casually strolled to the front of the room. "We're all monkeys with our fists trapped in the candy jar when it comes to Lemke's Treasure," he said. "Mankind has come so far in accomplishing the most difficult tasks, that he's forgotten how to use simple ingenuity to conquer the most mundane, most elemental – "

"Dr. Lemke?" Charysse interrupted softly, "There's actually seven hundred dollars here."

The class gasped. The teacher turned and saw what his students were staring at. On Charysse's desktop, thirty-five crumpled twenty-dollar bills sat on a wrinkled circle of plastic. Dr. Lemke went to Charysse's desk and picked up the plastic. He held it to the light and saw that it was perfectly intact. He examined the twine, and he saw that it too had not been damaged in any way, and was still tied in the knot he himself had made.

"Alright, Charysse!" Lotus clapped. The Raphael angels printed on her form-fitting top seemed to smile benevolently at Charysse's accomplishment.

"How did you get that thing open?" Bradley squeaked.

"Yes," Dr. Lemke said, nearly giggling with delight. "How did you conquer the mundane, my dear?"

"I did what you've been teaching us," Charysse explained while Dr. Lemke repackaged the money in the plastic bag. He pulled the knot even tighter this time. "I established and focused on my objective. I didn't think about the money." Dr. Lemke gave the bag back to Charysse, and she set about opening it the same way she had before. "Obtaining the contents of the bag wasn't my goal." She took the gathered edge of the plastic wrap and twisted it until it was narrower than the circumference of the bag's neck. "I kept it simpler than that. My goal was to open the bag according to your rules." As if pulling a ring from a finger, she slid the knot along the tight twist of plastic wrap. She opened the bag, smoothed out the wrinkles, and displayed the money.

"Bravo, Charysse," Dr. Lemke said.

Dr. Lemke had become one of her favorite instructors, and his praise meant a lot, but it was Shane's face Charysse sought. He looked at her, and he didn't have to use words to say how impressed he was. He showed it, in the way he smiled at her and slightly tipped his head in a bow.

"Talk about a monkey and a candy jar," came Mackenzie's voice from across the room.

Dressed in snug black pants, black boots and a fuzzy caramel top, Mackenzie sat with one leg hung over the other as she tapped the eraser end of a pencil on her desk. Her hair was pulled into a tight ponytail that made her eyes even more cat-shaped. As usual, she was aiming a poisonous smirk at Charysse. Mackenzie's verbal barbs were a regular part of Charysse's school day, and she ignored that one as she had all the others.

The bell rang for lunch and the students began to gather their belongings. "Another moment, please, class," Dr. Lemke announced. "I'm in need of a research assistant for a paper I wish to present at a symposium in Poland next month. The job basically entails writing up my notes into a coherent presentation. You won't be paid, however you will earn my eternal thanks and gratitude."

Several hands went up to volunteer.

"Charysse?" Dr. Lemke said.

She hiked her satchel onto her shoulder. "I didn't raise my hand, sir."

"Nonetheless, I wish to enlist your services."

"She's not interested," Mackenzie snapped, speaking over whatever Charysse might have said. Her backpack knocked Bradley back into his seat as she shoved her way past him to get closer to Dr. Lemke. "I was your assistant last semester. I'm the most familiar with your research style and your notes."

Dr. Lemke waited for his students, except for Charysse and Mackenzie, to exit the room before he addressed Mackenzie. "Miss Cole, your writing is technically perfect." Mackenzie smiled smugly. Charysse impatiently looked at her watch. "But Miss Cole, your writing lacks warmth and sensitivity. I'm afraid it lacks heart. I'm sorry, but I'd like Charysse to work with me on this project. There will be other papers, and you'll—"

Mackenzie stormed out of the room before Dr. Lemke could finish.

"I'm afraid you may have to pay the price for my rejection of Miss Cole's services, dear," Dr. Lemke said.

"It's okay," Charysse said with a shy smile. "I can pay for a lot of things with seven hundred dollars."

*

Marty and Candice had saved a seat for her at lunch, but Charysse was surprised to see that Lotus and Chrysanthemum weren't there.

"Lotus is getting a painting ready to send to some electronics company in Tokyo, and Chrys has a meeting with the school's lawyers," Marty told her. "Eichorn wants to revise its contract with Chrys. When her first book was published, the school only wanted a three-percent share of her royalties. Now that she's up for a Ruth Lilly Poetry fellowship, greedy ol' Eichorn wants seven percent of her book royalties."

"Wow," Charysse said, unpacking her lunch. "Maybe I should stop hustling trivia and write poetry."

"I heard about Lemke's Treasure," he said. "Way to go, doll."

"Thanks. It was weird. I was looking at the bag, and it seemed so obvious."

"That's the problem around here," Candice said between nibbles of an egg salad sandwich. "We're all so used to trying to solve complicated problems that we can't see our way through the simple ones."

"That's part of your thing, Charysse," Marty said. "You're really good at seeing things for what they are."

"What are you going to do with all that money?" Candice asked.

"Something fun, I think," Charysse said. "Maybe we could all go out to lunch or something."

"That would be cool," Candice grinned. "We could act like Beacon Hill trust fund babies out to tear up Lansdowne Street."

"Let's hire a limo," Marty said. "I used to do talk shows just because they always provided limousines to and from tapings."

"I've never been in one," Candice said.

"Then we'll get a limo," Charysse decided.

"Uh oh," Marty grumbled. "Trouble incoming, two o'clock."

Charysse looked up to see Mackenzie approaching their table. "Great," she mumbled. "I wonder what she wants now?"

Mackenzie stopped at the empty seat next to Candice. "Hi," she said, to Candice only. "Bea and Leslie and I are playing tennis at my house after school today. It's something we do every Friday. We need a fourth. Are you interested?"

Candice, her eyes round in surprise, only stared at Mackenzie. Charysse nudged her under the table, shaking her from her paralysis. "Uh," Candice worked out, "um…tennis? With you and your friends?"

Mackenzie laughed. It sounded like the rustle of dead leaves in a weak breeze. "Well, they're your friends, too, Candy, it's not like we're strangers. Why don't you come on over to my table, and I'll tell you what to bring."

"I've never played tennis before in my life," Candice said as she shoved the remnants of her lunch into her insulated lunch sack.

"That's okay," Mackenzie said. "Bea sucks, too."

"See you, guys," Candice called over her shoulder as Mackenzie put an arm around her waist and guided her to the table where Bea and Leslie sat.

"'*Candy?*'" Charysse repeated.

"Big Mac's a liar," Marty said. "She has no friends. Bea and Leslie hang around her because they're scared not to. And now she's trying to lure Candice to the Dark Side."

"It's just a tennis date."

"This was the first time—*ever*—that Mackenzie has spoken to Candice as if she were a human being. Mac's trying to build up her army."

"Well, Candice is smart enough to know that she's being used, if that's the case." Charysse peeked at Candice, who was now sitting between blonde Bea and dark-haired Leslie, with Mackenzie standing over her. The girls were laughing and pointing at something in a magazine. Candice's laughter came a couple of beats after the other girls'.

"You give Candice too much credit," Marty scoffed. "She's not like us. She's a Transfer who's always wanted to run with the Natives."

"It's about time Candice made other friends. If she doesn't like them, she can always come back to us."

Marty shook his head and took out a felt-tip pen. He pushed his lunch tray aside and began drawing on the tabletop, adding more squiggles and turns to the maze he'd begun on the first day of school. "Don't say I didn't warn you," he said somberly.

*

Candice was gone, replaced by 'Candy,' who spent all of her free time as the fourth in the Mackenzie Cole quartet. Charysse, Marty and the Achearn twins missed Candice's company during lunch hour.

"Big Mac represents everything Candice wants to be," Lotus said quietly over her untouched lentil soup. "She's not strong enough to fight Mackenzie's gravitational pull."

"Mackenzie only wanted Candice to be in her circle because she was friends with you, Charysse," Chrysanthemum said, her nose in the pages of *A Case of Curiosities*. "She knew she'd never be able to get me or Lotus to run after her like a pet monkey."

Charysse quietly ate her lunch while she looked at Candice. Candy, now. Along with her name, her wardrobe had changed in the past week. Instead of her usual neutral colors and styles, she now wore a miniskirt and tight top that emphasized her worst features, rather than flattered them. Her brown hair had been dyed a banana-blond that completely washed out her skin. Even worse was her hairstyle, an off-center ponytail that worked on Mackenzie, but made Candice look like a Picasso.

"That's so sad," Lotus said. "If she was going to sponge up someone else's personality, why did she have to pick Mackenzie Cole's?"

Marty looked up from his maze and stared beyond the three girls. "Well, look who decided to come down from the collegiate mountain today."

Charysse peered over her shoulder and saw Shane. He wore jeans and a black sweater with the collar of a white T-shirt peeking from the neck. He hadn't made any further inquiries regarding her after hours plans since the first day of school, when he'd been interrupted. They had talked before and after classes, but the chit-chat never went deeper than discussing homework assignments or something interesting they'd read on the Internet or seen on cable – it was the sort of talk Charysse figured people initiated just to have an excuse to hear each other's voices. And to look into their eyes. And to watch their mouths shape words.

She sat straighter in her chair, but tried to make no other outward signs that she was glad to see him. Her skin prickled, as though his presence generated an electric charge that bounced off her nerve endings. He seemed to have that effect on every girl in the room, most of them turning to stare at him as he passed. Mackenzie left her table and attempted an interception, almost tripping over the thick soles of her shoes as she tried to keep up with his long strides while chattering non-stop. Shane, his eyes on Charysse, simply stepped around Mackenzie and headed directly for the Transfers table. Charysse, biting back an excited smile, didn't look away until he was standing beside her.

"Hi, Shane," Lotus and Chrysanthemum harmonized as he came to a stop.

"Mind if I join you guys?" he asked.

Lotus cleared her sketchbook from the place between her and Charysse. "Not at all."

"Please, do," said Chrysanthemum, who actually closed her book and hastily reached past her sister to pull her backpack from the chair.

Marty shook his head at the gooey expressions of his female tablemates. "If you must," he grudgingly said to Shane. "What brings you 'round these here parts, Maverick?"

"My math class is cancelled." Shane took the freshly emptied chair between Charysse and Lotus and turned it around backwards. He straddled it and sat, resting his forearms over the back of the chair. "My prof is out of town attending a conference on Fractal Geometry."

"What the frac are you talking about?" Marty asked.

"Fractal geometry," Charysse murmured thoughtfully. "Non-integer dimensions?"

Shane's eyes seemed to roam over her face, sparking a furious blush everywhere his gaze landed. He gave her a quiet smile that reduced the population of the crowded cafeteria to two. "The dimension between two whole numbers."

Her expression intensified as she tried to visualize his description. All at once, her features relaxed with understanding. "A fractal curve lies between the first and second dimension depending on how much space it occupies as it curves and twists."

"Right," Shane said, smiling. "A hill-shaped plane covered in bumps is closer to the second dimension, but if you flatten the plane and make the bumps bigger, the plane would be closer to the third dimension."

"Uh," Lotus began, "is this a private conversation? 'Cause sis and Marty and I can frac off if you two want to break bread duo-like."

Shane shook himself and returned his attention to the whole table. "What's good today?"

Marty's upper lip curled as he cast a glance at his lunch tray. "Crandall's F-Cube is better than this stuff."

"I've got half a turkey sandwich up for grabs," Charysse said. She passed it to him.

"Thanks." Shane didn't take the thick sandwich immediately. He spent a moment staring at her, watching her profile as she chewed.

"Lancelot waltzes in and gets fed and you leave me to the mercy of the cafeteria's macrobiotic meatless balls?" Marty accused.

"You already ate most of my antipasto salad and my oatmeal raisin cookies," Charysse pointed out. She handed the last of her big, soft cookies to Shane.

"This sandwich looks awesome." He lifted one end of the soft roll to peek at the filling, and then he took a huge bite. "What's this stuff?"

"It's a DiGregorio family recipe," Charysse said. "Roasted red peppers, roasted garlic, olives, red onion and hearts of palm minced and mixed with fresh ground black pepper and a little olive oil."

"Little Emeril likes to cook." Marty tossed a thumb at Shane. "Just yesterday he was in the cafeteria trading casserole recipes with Mrs. Grundy."

"A Scottish chef?" Charysse said. "That's a rarity."

"My mother is Italian. I get my love of good food from her."

"Does your mom have any new books coming out soon?" Marty asked.

Shane slowly stopped chewing. "No." The light in his eyes dimmed as he set down the sandwich. "The prof's away but I still have assignments due." He rose from the chair and grabbed his backpack from the floor. "I need to get to the Math Lab. I'll see you guys in Lindy's class."

"Touchy," Marty said, snagging the remains of Shane's sandwich.

"That was weird," Lotus observed.

"His mom is a writer?" Charysse asked.

"Adrianna Salerno McKenna," Chrysanthemum said. "Author of twenty books. Perhaps you've heard of *Song For My Children*?"

"Who hasn't? That's one of my mom's favorites," Charysse said. "That book left her bawling for a week. She wrote a passage from it in the card she gave me for my sixteenth birthday. The movie wasn't as good as the book, though."

"Maybe that's what made Shane's mom sick." Marty gobbled up Shane's cookie.

"She's ill?"

"That's the story that made the rounds a couple of years ago," Chrysanthemum said. "She hasn't published anything in five years."

"What's she got?" Charysse asked.

Marty shrugged. "Who knows? Shane keeps it locked up tight."

Charysse only half listened as Marty and the twins chatted through the rest of their lunch hour. Her thoughts were fixed on Shane, the reason for his sudden departure, and whether he'd lost the spark of interest he'd shown in her on the first day of school. Her spark for him still burned, and occasionally threatened to flare out of control.

There had been times, like when she'd earned Lemke's Treasure, when he looked at her and she was convinced that he was just as interested in her as she was in him. But there were other times, like now, when she thought he was just a nice boy being kind to the new girl.

Donovan Rainey had been driving her home since the second day of school, and she had tried to get information from him about Shane's dating status. But Donovan was always more interested in talking about himself. Charysse realized that if she wanted to know more about Shane, she would just have to go directly to the source.

After Lindy's class, she stood next to Shane and watched as he fastened his backpack. "I'm not doing anything," she said when he finally noticed her.

"What?" he chuckled softly.

"You asked me what I was doing after school. I'm not doing anything."

"That was seven weeks ago." He slung his pack over his right shoulder. "I thought you and Donovan were hanging out."

"He lives near me. We carpool in the afternoons because I get home too late when I take the T. It's strictly a business arrangement. I pay him for gas, and he spends the time me-deep in conversation and chain-smoking hand-rolled cigarettes."

Shane laughed, and Charysse felt more at ease. "Have you had the official tour?"

"Mr. Kennedy took me around when—"

"How would you like the unauthorized tour of Eichorn?" he cut in.

"I think I'd like that very much." She smiled, and when Shane smiled back, she wondered how she could possibly tour anything when her feet no longer touched the floor.

*

"This is Señora Olazabal's Spanish class," Shane said. Charysse felt the brush of his hand at the small of her back as he ushered her into the empty classroom. "It's the only foreign language class taught on the first floor."

Every day, Charysse climbed eight flights of stairs to get to her French class, so she knew that all the other foreign language courses were taught on the penthouse level of the Main Building. "Is Señora Olazabal afraid of heights?"

"It's because of Norm Webber." Shane hung his thumbs through the empty belt loops of his jeans. "Sometimes he freaks out. When he has to actually speak to people in class, he freaks so bad, he jumps out of the window. He started that back at Corcoran. Corcoran's all one level, but when he got to Busch, he broke his ankle when he jumped out of a second-story window to get out of having to give a speech on Cervantes. Eichorn got the jump on him, so to speak, by putting his class on the ground floor."

"Where does he go after he jumps out of the window?" Charysse reached up and set a pineapple-shaped piñata gently swinging. She noticed that Shane's eyes had dropped to her midriff, which was modestly bared by her raised arms. A raging blush stung her face as she carefully shoved her hands into the pockets of her jeans.

"Usually he hides in the Math Lab." Shane moved toward the door and Charysse followed him. "He's gotten better over time. Freshman year, he used to run all the way home."

"Where does he live?" Charysse was conscious of the way Shane's arm made contact with hers as they walked down the empty corridor.

"Quincy."

"That's about twenty-five miles away," Charysse chuckled. "Norm's our resident cross-country champ, too."

He took her to the cafeteria and showed her the spot where a former boys assistant coach literally lost his lunch after an Eichorn grad's experiment with fungus mysteriously ended up in the Salad Bar. He took her to the Music Building and showed her the "furry" ceiling of Dr. Lithgow's office. The department head had shot hundreds of rubber bands at the tiny squares in the grids covering the fluorescent light fixtures. The rubber bands dangled, giving the ceiling the appearance of shaggy brown fur. Charysse realized that Shane saved the best for last when he led her into the sand dunes of Eichorn's desert.

"This is the greenhouse." He took her hand to help her down the steep first step. She pressed back a smile when he made no effort to release her hand once she had safely navigated it. "It's one hundred and eighty yards long and forty feet at its highest point. There are three climates. Desert, temperate and tropical. The desert is maintained at one hundred and ten degrees during the day, but the temperature drops to about half that at night."

"This is amazing." Charysse stooped and scooped up a handful of soft, powdery sand. Like fine sugar it sifted through her fingers as she scanned her surroundings. The place looked like the pictures she'd seen of the Arizona deserts, with a variety of cacti and short, sturdy green foliage. She half expected to see Wile E. Coyote chasing the Road Runner from behind one of the giant, redstone boulders situated near one arched wall of the greenhouse.

Charysse used her free hand to mop her forehead. Twenty seconds into the place and she was already perspiring. Shane led her deeper into the greenhouse and through a set of automatic doors. She took a deep breath of the cooler air in this section, where green grass and deciduous trees replaced the bright, hot, bare environment of the desert. Like the trees outside the greenhouse, the oaks, elms, sycamores and birches in this temperate region were in the middle of showy changes of color. Charysse noticed work stands and tables covered with lab equipment that appeared to measure and monitor water and soil samples.

Shane guided her along a narrow path that took them beneath a wide pergola heavy with tiny, perfectly round, purplish-red grapes. "It's so pretty here," Charysse remarked. "I feel like I'm in Italy or something. What do you do with the grapes?"

The thick covering of grape leaves and clusters closed out much of the light, leaving the flagstones dappled in shadows. Shane stopped, stood on his tiptoes, and picked a cluster of grapes. He set them in her hand and she held them to her nose, inhaling deeply. "They smell so good."

"They're Professor Roentgen's hybrid. She combined a really sweet Muscat grape with a red Japanese grape and got these." He stood so close to her that the front of his shirt brushed the backs of her fingers, which were slightly closed around the grapes. He took one of the grapes and offered it to her. "Try one."

She was more aware of the light glance of his fingertip across her lower lip than the smooth skin of the grape, until her teeth closed on it. Her eyes widened as the thick, sweet juice of the grape ran over her tongue.

"Holy cow," she exclaimed, popping two more grapes into her mouth. "These are the best grapes I've ever tasted."

"Professor Roentgen sells them to gourmet restaurants for twenty dollars a pound. We get them for free because we're students. But we can only eat them at school."

"Fair enough, I guess. Want some?" She dangled the bunch high above his mouth as they continued beneath the pergola. Shane caught a few grapes in his teeth and noisily chomped them. When she teased him by holding them farther out of reach, he tickled her, making her lower them. Charysse laughed until tears ran from her eyes as he put one arm around her and held her wrist with his other hand, holding the grapes in place so he could devour the bunch Cookie Monster-style.

"You've got grape juice on your chin," she told him, her laughter tapering off. Both of his hands had found their way to her waist and they tightened there for an instant before he dropped them and used the bottom of his sweater to wipe his face.

"Is that better?"

She nodded, her eyes fixed on his. There was just enough shadowy light under the pergola for her to see the way he studied her face, particularly her lips. Boys had looked at her before, but never the way Shane looked at her now, in the lovely solitude of the grape arbor. If she had Bonnie's courage, she would have made use of that moment by finding out if Professor Roentgen's hybrid grapes tasted as good on Shane's lips as they had on hers.

But she wasn't Bonnie. "What's next?" she asked.

"How about paradise?" He gave her a tiny smile that made her wish she were Bonnie even more as he took her hand and led her into the last part of the greenhouse.

As amazing as the other two sections had been, the tropical rainforest truly was paradise. Dense, colorful foliage filled the place and threatened to overrun the pathway. Charysse filled in the sounds of monkeys and macaws in her mind, because that was all that was missing to transform the place completely to a piece of the Amazon rainforest. The sound of rushing water grew louder as Shane pushed aside the giant leaves of Elephant ear plants and thick, hanging vines to show her the artificial waterfall that generated the greenhouse's power.

The water began atop a four-story cliff and hammered down into a narrow river full of vegetation and darting tropical fish. The drumming of the waterfall was loud, and Shane had to bow his head to place his ear near her mouth to hear her speak. "Are those orchids?" she asked, pointing to distant tables supporting rows and rows of peculiar, delicate plants.

"The junior class grows them," Shane answered, his voice humming in her head. She closed her eyes and tipped her head more toward his lips, which were feathery and light against the shell of her ear. "Every June they grow them for weddings. That's how they pay for their class party at the end of the year."

"Do you have some kind of research or money-making venture in the greenhouse?"

He shook his head. "I just like it here."

"So it's your escape." She lifted her face to his, and her blood surged at his proximity.

"It can be yours, too. I'm willing to share it."

She smiled. "Your hair is starting to curl."

"So's yours." He tweaked the end of a lock of her hair. It spiraled around his finger.

"It's the humidity," she said. "It makes my hair frizz."

"Do you want to go?" He took a few steps away from the waterfall.

"Absolutely not. But I can barely hear you over the water."

Charysse let him guide her to the thick trunk of a tree with gnarled roots that looked like one of Marty's mazes. They were far enough from the waterfall to enjoy the sight of it without being overwhelmed by its powerful voice.

"Actually, I probably should get going," she said. "I was supposed to call my friend Bonnie when I got home. We haven't seen much of each other since school started. I have so much more homework now, I've missed the last three Sundae Sundays. We've known each other since we were eight, and I feel like we're becoming strangers." Charysse chuckled sadly. "She thinks Dr. Charles Xavier runs the school and we're all mutants. Hopefully we can catch up on Saturday. Every year, Bonnie has a Halloween sleepover. We get loaded up on HoHo's, candy corn and cheese puffs and watch terrible horror movies. It sounds stupid, but it's really fun."

"Maybe you could bring her to Eichorn to visit some day. Give her a chance to see that we're just regular people. Well, on the outside, anyway. The only reason I take math at Wellington is so I can have a life outside of Eichorn," Shane said. "It's a trade-off. I make my parents happy by taking Fractal Geometry at Wellington, they make me happy by letting me do something I'm actually interested in."

Shane scaled the tree's roots. He took Charysse's hand and helped her find a comfortable perch beside him. She stared at him for a moment before she said, "Like football?"

"Cross-country, debate and chess are pretty much the only competitive sports Eichorn offers, so I joined an adult weekend football league." He did a double take. "How did you know?" he grinned. "I didn't tell anybody at Eichorn."

She tapped her forehead.

"Yes, I've seen for myself that you're 'wicket smaht.'"

"*Your* forehead," she clarified. She plucked a tiny leaf from the mossy trunk of the tree. "The scratch. It looks like you butted helmets with someone."

"I like the way you notice things," he said. "And the way you see them."

"Ms. Lindy says that I'm an Observer. She says that's part of my 'genius.'"

"Ms. Lindy's a weird cat. She's the reason all my exams are custom-tailored."

"I've been meaning to ask you about that." Charysse put her back to the tree trunk. "I saw that your American History exam was in essay form but the rest of us had multiple choice tests."

He looked away from her before turning his gaze to the leaf he twirled between his fingers. "I have an eidetic memory. Ms. Lindy worries that I don't actually learn things because it's easier to just remember without real comprehension. My tests are designed to force me to actually assimilate, analyze and process the info I take in, rather than just spit it out on command."

"You make yourself sound like a computer. There's nothing wrong with having a photographic memory."

He stared at his leaf. "I know."

"Are you ashamed of it?"

"No."

"How good are you?"

"When I was four, I memorized the Boston Red Sox Media Guide. I know it to this day."

"Wow. You must have been a big baseball fan back then."

"Don't confuse interest with mindless aptitude." Shane's mood seemed to darken to match the twilight sky.

"What's the difference? If you're interested in something, whether it's Fractal Geometry or U2's Greatest Hits, learning about it is cake."

"When you're beautiful, people say, 'You should be a model,'" he argued. "If you tell good stories, people say, 'You should be a writer.' When you're smart, or a freak like me, you're supposed to cure cancer. You're supposed to save the world. The keys are up here." He jabbed a finger into his right temple. "How to end world hunger. How to create world peace. How to turn water into gas and tin foil into gold. The curse of expectation is on you now, too."

"I've always expected a lot from myself, Shane," she said. "I wanted to come to Eichorn because I wanted the chance to match my expectations with opportunity. Maybe I see things differently because I'm not a so-called Native. I've seen that intelligence comes in lots of forms and flavors. There's a guy at Lesterville who's been left back twice, but he can build Corvette engines from scratch. There's a waitress at Pizzazz Pizza who knows every country song ever recorded. She knows the songwriter, the singers, the albums the songs are on—"

"It's easier for people like them," Shane said. "They do what they do because they want to. They don't have to deal with obligation the way we do."

"It's not expectation or obligation that gets to you, Shane. It's guilt."

"How do you figure that?"

"You're capable of so much, but not the thing you most want."

He looked at her, thoroughly confused. "And I suppose you know what I want?"

"No. But when I do, I'll tell you." His quiet made her look at her watch. It was past six, and she had a Chemistry exam to study for along with the new assignment of being Dr. Lemke's research assistant. She stood. "I have to get going, Shane. If I don't catch the last train, I'll have to spend the night here."

"I'll take you home," he offered, brushing off the seat of his jeans as he rose.

"Where do you live?" she asked.

"On Lawrence Street. Here in Wakefield."

"That's seven blocks from school. Lesterville is forty minutes out of your way."

"It's a nice night for a drive. It's no problem, Charysse. I want to take you home."

"Why?"

His fingers moved delicately through her hair as he plucked tiny pink and white petals from it. "Because I'm not ready to say goodnight to you yet."

Chapter Four

Just after dark on Halloween, Charysse dialed Bonnie's number as she rushed around her room, looking for the bottoms to her favorite plaid flannel pajamas. Bonnie's room tended to be a little drafty, and Halloween had a wintry feel to it with temperatures expected to dive into the high teens.

"Hey, Bonnie!" Charysse said cheerfully when Bonnie answered her phone. "One of my professors asked me to write his notes into a paper for him, so I had to do some fact-checking this afternoon. I got a late start, but I got everything I needed. I'm packing now, and I can be there in ten minutes, if—"

"The girls are already here," Bonnie said flatly.

Charysse now heard the muffled voices in the background. One of them became louder and clearer. "Is that Charysse?" it asked.

"Yeah," Bonnie said.

Charysse thought Bonnie couldn't have sounded more disinterested if she had tried.

"Tell her I said, 'Hi, I.Q.,'" the voice said with a laugh. "Get it? *Hi* I.Q.?"

The voices in the background laughed and shouted their hellos to Charysse, all but Bonnie.

"I guess the party's already started," Charysse said. She sat heavily on the edge of her bed.

"I guess so."

"Is this how it ends for us, Bonnie?"

"You're the one who doesn't return phone calls," Bonnie accused. "You're the one who's too busy with the fancy new school and the new smart friends."

"You're not being fair and you know it," Charysse argued. "You know how much work I have now."

"Yeah, too much work to be bothered with Lesterville crud like me."

"Don't put words in my mouth."

"How could I? I probably couldn't pronounce the big, fancy words you'd use!"

"If you don't want me at your party, that's fine." Charysse shut her eyes tight, determined not to cry. "But remember that you were the one who shut me out, Bonnie, not the other way around."

"Fine," Bonnie said indifferently. "I don't want you at my party."

"Fine," Charysse snapped.

"Fine!" Bonnie shouted.

Both girls hung up the phone at the same time. Charysse sat on her bed a moment longer, her arms crossed angrily over her chest. She had the car because her mother had left it for her, thinking that she would need it to get to Bonnie's pajama party. Charysse rarely got the car for the night, and she didn't want to waste the occasion. By the time she'd put on her coat, grabbed the car keys and climbed into the driver's seat of her mother's late model Toyota, Charysse had decided where she wanted to go for Halloween.

*

"Trick or Treat!"

A little boy dressed in a silvery-green iridescent alien costume squealed the words through the bug-eyed mask that covered him from head to mid-chest when he opened the door for Charysse.

"That's supposed to be my line," Charysse said.

"Huh?" said the miniature alien.

Charysse bent over, to meet the alien's shiny black eyes. She could just make out chubby smiling cheeks within the dark-tinted plastic. "I'm supposed to say Trick or Treat. Then you're supposed to decide what it is you want. A trick, or a treat."

The alien held out his hand. "I want a treat."

"I don't have any treats but I know a trick," Charysse offered.

"Okay," the alien said.

The egg-shaped eyes of his mask followed Charysse's movements as she showed him her empty hands, palms forward. She flicked her right hand, and a dollar bill appeared from thin air. She closed her hands and tapped her fists together. She opened her left fist, and the dollar bill was there in her hand.

"Cool!" the alien cooed.

Charysse tossed both hands in the air, and the dollar disappeared.

"Where'd it go?" the alien asked.

"I don't know," Charysse said. She pointed to the bowl full of candy he still clutched in his three-fingered alien paws. "Could I have a candy bar?"

"Sure." The alien slipped his hand out of his glove and picked up a miniature chocolate bar. "No way!" he laughed when he saw the dollar bill poking from the middle of the bowl.

"That's a good trick," said a big, burly man dressed as the Red Sox-era Babe Ruth. He stood behind the boy. "Give her back her money, son."

"Magic dollars belong to whoever finds them," Charysse said. "You must be Mr. Kosh, Marty's dad." Charysse offered her hand.

"The one and only," Mr. Kosh said. "And you are ... ?"

"Charysse DiGregorio. I'm – "

"The new girl," Mr. Kosh said, his large, meaty hand swallowing hers and giving it a good shake. "Marty has told us a lot about you."

"He talks about you all the time," the alien complained wearily.

"Scoot." Mr. Kosh helped his son along by giving him a gentle push with the end of his Louisville Slugger. "Come on in, Charysse. Marty's in his maze."

Charysse wondered about Mr. Kosh's statement as he showed her into the bright, open kitchen of the big Victorian. The entire Kosh family, Marty's mom dressed as Marie Curie, and Marty's three brothers—the alien, a ninja and a junior version of Pedro Martinez—were gathered around the blonde circle of a table covered with candy. Mrs. Kosh sorted through the respective piles, discarding anything that wasn't wrapped or had suspicious breaks in the packaging.

"Honey," Mr. Kosh said, standing near his wife, "this is Charysse. Marty's friend."

"I'm pleased to finally meet you," Mrs. Kosh said. "Marty has spoken of you so often that—"

"You are so hot!" the ninja said, his wide brown eyes glued to a point somewhere below Charysse's neck. Charysse put the boy's age at about thirteen or fourteen. Nothing else could explain why he'd be so impressed by her simple black shirt and jacket, and blue jeans.

"Knock it off, you little animal," Mr. Kosh muttered.

"You're so pretty. I can't believe you go to Eichorn," the ninja persisted.

"I lot of pretty girls go to Eichorn," Charysse said.

"Yeah," grunted Pedro, "pretty ugmo."

"Joe and Ted, would you two like to spend the rest of the weekend without video games?" Mrs. Kosh asked.

"No," the boys said in unison.

"Then cut the cave boy crap and one of you take Charysse to Marty."

The ninja and Pedro were still wrestling over who got to be Charysse's escort when the alien hopped off of his chair and took Charysse's hand. He pulled her through the kitchen and through the back door. He took her beyond the deck, the swimming pool and the two-car garage to a building that looked like a small warehouse.

"Marty's in his maze," the alien said.

"That's what your dad said," Charysse remarked. "What's your name, by the way?"

"Michael," he said. "But everyone calls me Mickey."

"Ted, Joe and Mickey," Charysse said. "All famous baseball players."

"My dad's a sportswriter for the *Herald*," Mickey said. "He loves baseball."

"Who's Marty named after?"

"My grandpa. He wasn't a baseball player, though. He was a doctor."

"What did you mean when you said Marty was 'in' his maze?"

Mickey pulled off his mask and used his upper arm to wipe his sweaty forehead. With the moonlight shining on his cherubic face, Charysse saw that Mickey was about six or seven years old.

"Marty's a psycho," Mickey said.

"If that were true, I wouldn't be here," Charysse said.

"Maybe you're a psycho, too."

"What school do you go to?"

"Corcoran," Mickey said sullenly.

"Where do Ted and Joe go?"

"They're at Wakefield High. Ted's a freshman, Joe's a sophomore."

"Go Warriors," Charysse said.

"You look like a cheerleader, you know," Mickey stated sagely.

"I liked it better when you called me a psycho."

Mickey pressed a small white button.

"Who is it?" Marty's impatient voice came through the intercom mounted above the doorbell.

"Your friend Charysse is here." Mickey had to stand on his tiptoes to speak into the intercom.

A few seconds later, the heavy steel door swung open. Charysse was pulled into the dark building while Mickey was shoved a step back by his forehead. Once the door closed, the lights came up. Marty was dressed in a pair of grubby overalls. His hands, bare arms and shoulders and face were smudged with grime. "What are you?" Charysse asked. "Mike the Mechanic?" Marty treated her to one of his enigmatic little smiles and led her into the warehouse. "Good Charlotte," Charysse gasped, staring at the sight before her. "What is that?"

Twists, turns and knots of connected pipes almost entirely filled the immense space. The dark gray aluminum pipes looked just like the ones in Charysse's basement, the ones that connected her furnace to the heating system. Marty's monumental maze was two stories tall and at least fifty yards long.

"This is my maze," Marty said. He squatted over a big toolbox and rooted through it. He took out a long monkey wrench and took it with him when he entered the maze and climbed up to a section close to the ceiling. The lean muscles of his arms and shoulders flexed as he tightened a ring clamp that joined two sections of pipe.

Marty seemed different than how he was at school. He was relaxed, focused and serious as he moved around his maze with the agility of a spider in its web. In his element, surrounded by his three-dimensional opus, it was as though his true self was revealed. "How long have you been working on this?" Charysse asked.

"It'll be seven years in June."

"Does it have a solution?"

"Not yet. But it will when it's finished." He grimaced as he wrenched a piece of pipe into the shape he wanted it in. "I thought you had your annual pajama party tonight."

"Bonnie and I are fighting," Charysse admitted. She stepped closer to the maze and ran her hand along a length of pipe. "She's mad because she thinks I've put Eichorn ahead of her in my life."

"You did," Marty said simply.

"No I didn't," Charysse protested.

"You used to talk about Bonnie all the time. Now you only talk about school."

Charysse pondered Marty's observation. "I like school," she said. "Marty, I feel like I've been released from prison after serving time for a crime I didn't commit. I was so bored at Lesterville. Some of my teachers tried to keep me challenged, but it wasn't enough. Eichorn is almost too much sometimes, and I really like that. No one calls me Encyclopedia Head or trashes my locker for ruining a curve."

Marty stopped working. "And you have a boyfriend."

"No, I don't," she chuckled nervously. She removed her denim jacket and laid it across a countertop cluttered with tools.

Marty sat on one pipe and rested his forearms across another piece. "Then climb up here and kiss me."

"Marty!"

"Then I'll come down to you." He climbed down the outside of the structure before leaping from it. He landed heavily in his dirty work books. He clomped across the concrete floor.

Charysse stepped back as he neared her, until she backed into some of Marty's welding equipment. She stepped to the side and found her back pressing against a bare wall.

"Marty, what are you doing?"

He stopped an inch away from her. He flattened one hand on the wall, his arm barring her from moving to the right. He gave her a lazy smile. The familiar flicker of mischief in his eyes made Charysse smile. "Have you lost your A-Mazing mind?" she asked.

"I realize that this is probably the last chance I'll ever have to kiss you." His eyes followed hers, refusing to let her break their shared gaze. "I mean, what's a little smooch between friends, Charysse? Especially if there's no one else you have any special feelings for."

She ducked under his arm. "You seem to have thought this through."

He turned to face her. "I've wanted to kiss you since the first day of school. At first it was just a physical thing."

"Cave boy."

"But then I got to know you and ... I just really want to know what it would be like to kiss you."

"Marty, I don't know what to say."

"I do." He leaned against the wall, one ankle crossed over the other. "You like me as a friend. I've seen you and Shane dance, Charysse. I've seen the way you look at him. He looks at you the same way. Part of the reason you like school is because you like Shane, too. Bonnie, naturally, takes a backseat to that." Marty moved to the counter lining the wall. Under his breath, he said, "But of course, if Bonnie ever met Shane, she'd probably be crazy about him, too."

Charysse approached him. "Actually, you're more Bonnie's type than Shane is."

"Yeah?" Marty didn't turn away from the odds and ends of metal he sorted through on the counter, but Charysse caught a glimpse of his tiny smile.

"She likes guys who are good with their hands."

"So when are you going to kiss and makeup so I can meet her?" He turned around. "And can I be there to watch?"

"Bonnie and I never stay mad at each other for long. I'll call her when I get home. How come you haven't asked me what she looks like?"

Marty lifted a shoulder in a confident shrug. "I already know. She's beautiful."

"How do you know that?"

Golden sparks flashed in Marty's green eyes. "All girls are beautiful."

*

Charysse and Bonnie, giggling low, straggled into Ms. Lindy's class. Charysse led Bonnie to the teacher's desk. "You look bright today," Charysse said, commenting on Ms. Lindy's lemon-yellow blouse.

"I needed a break from Norm," she explained. "Yellow is a high anxiety color. Norm hasn't come within two hundred feet of me today."

"That's like the time Mr. Creedy got hair implants," Bonnie remarked, referring to the homeroom teacher she and Charysse had for junior year. "They were so bad, they looked like they'd been screwed into his head. I got the creeps every time he came near me."

Ms. Lindy laughed out loud at the image Bonnie's description conjured. "Ms. Lindy," Charysse said, "I'd like you to meet Bonita Gagliardi, my best friend. Since we're open on Veteran's Day while every other school in the tri-state area is closed, I thought today would be a good day for Bonnie to visit."

"Good to meet you, ma'am." Bonnie shook Ms. Lindy's hand. "Charysse says you're the coolest teacher at I.Q. Uh ... Eichorn. Sorry."

Ms. Lindy waved a dismissive hand. "We've been called worse. Have you enjoyed your visit, Bonnie?"

"Well, to tell you the truth, it's not quite what I expected." Bonnie sat on the edge of Ms. Lindy's desk. She crossed her legs. The opalescent beads on the ends of her shoelaces clicked and clattered as she swung her pink-sneakered feet. "I visited the Performing Arts High School in Boston and all the kids were dancin' and playin' their instruments in the hallways. I visited a Catholic High school once, and saw all these Jesuses hangin' everywhere and all these statues of the Blessed Virgin Mary."

Charysse glanced at Ms. Lindy. She was pleased to see her teacher's appreciative smile and attentive gaze at Bonnie. In the course of Bonnie's day, some of the other teachers had been disinterested to the point of rudeness.

"What did you expect to see here?" Ms. Lindy asked.

Bonnie leaned closer to the teacher. "Dexter's laboratory, basically. A bunch of computer heads walking into walls. I only saw one of those."

"Norm," Charysse said.

"Everybody else seems pretty normal, I guess," Bonnie said. "I got a kick outta that Laser Alarm in Char's science class."

"Henry Dashiell's BioRhythm Sensor," Charysse said.

"It's wicked cool," Bonnie said. She began to chew her omnipresent gum with more exuberance. "Hank – "

"Hank?" Ms. Lindy raised an eyebrow at Charysse.

"Henry let her call him Hank," Charysse said.

"Let me finish," Bonnie said. "Hank explained the whole thing to me. He says that every person's got their own electricity."

A snorting laugh sounded from the rear corner of the room. Charysse turned to see Mackenzie and Candice sitting face to face in a pair of desks. Mackenzie made an exaggerated attempt to cover her snickering laughter with her hand. Candice's sad eyes met Charysse's, and she forced herself to laugh, too, after Mackenzie gave her a sharp shove.

Bonnie ignored the laughter, if she heard it at all. "So Hank hooked me up to his thingamajig ... what did he call it? Oh yeah, his cardiopulmonary electrowhoziewhatzit. So he programs my electricity into his machine, and he turns it on. There's six blue lines that criss-cross each other, like in that movie, *Entrapment*, when Catherine Zeta-Jones is practicin' stealing that ugly mask." Bonnie stopped to breathe before continuing. "So I walk through the lasers. I thought I was gonna get zapped, but nothing happened. Charysse walks through, and this alarm goes off, and it was loud! I mean, I bet my Grandma Sadie in Bridgewater heard that thing, and she's part deaf. No lie. Hank's

67

seriously on to something with that Biorhythm alarm. He should make them and sell them or something."

Marty, who had been at his desk simply watching Bonnie, joined her at Ms. Lindy's desk. "'Hank' has six patents already," he told Bonnie. "He's big on the electrical inventions. He's been shocked at least ten times, playing with the stuff."

"Eight," Bonnie said. Her feet stilled as a wide smile bloomed on her face. "Hank told me all about them. He's got lots of good stories."

"I'll bet," Marty said.

"Do you have any good stories, Marty?"

Bonnie had switched gears and was now in flirtation mode. It was working, if the emerald fire in Marty's eyes was a fair indication.

"None as jolting as Hank's," he said. "I saved seats for you guys." He offered a hand to Bonnie. She took it, though she didn't really need help hopping off of Ms. Lindy's desk.

Charysse followed the couple. She wondered where Shane was as Bonnie sat in the desk beside Marty's. She'd last seen him in Calculus, where he functioned more as a teaching assistant than a regular student. She had introduced him to Bonnie in the spare moments after class, but he'd had to rush off to Wellington. She'd been looking forward to Lindy's class, when he could get the full Bonnie experience.

"Who's your friend?"

Charysse tore her eyes from the door to see Mackenzie and Candice standing near Bonnie.

"Don't tell me," Mackenzie said. "This is your best bud from Lesterville."

Bonnie giggled and plucked at the bright red LESTERVILLE emblazoned on the front of her sweatshirt. "Some genius." She sat back in her seat and stared up at Mackenzie. "What gave me away?"

"What didn't," Mackenzie smirked.

"You must be Mackenzie Cole," Bonnie said. "Char's told me a lot about you."

"All good, I'm sure." Mackenzie narrowed her eyes at Charysse.

"She said you were tall," Bonnie laughed. "She was right."

Mackenzie gave Bonnie a last look of distaste before turning to Charysse. "I was wondering how you were doing with Dr. Lemke's notes."

"Fine," Charysse said. "Good. Thanks for asking." With a little shake of her head, Charysse turned back to Bonnie and Marty.

"Dr. Lemke is very particular about his papers," Mackenzie went on. "I know yours is due on Friday, so I'd be happy to proofread your work for you. A fresh pair of eyes can always catch little mistakes. And big ones, of course."

Charysse avoided Bonnie's gaze. If she looked at Bonnie, she knew she would start laughing right in Mackenzie's face. "Is she frickin' kiddin'?" Bonnie asked. "You don't need anybody checkin' on your work, Char."

"You never give up, do you, Mac?" Marty said.

"Charysse?" Mackenzie said impatiently.

"Mackenzie, I appreciate your offer, and while your writing skills are technically perfect, I'd rather walk through school naked than have you anywhere near my Lemke paper."

"Suit yourself!" Mackenzie spat the two words between her clenched teeth. She went back to her desk in an angry swirl of leather jacket and wool skirt.

"Candice, I haven't introduced you to my friend, Bonnie," Charysse started.

"Candice!" Mackenzie hissed.

Candice jumped. "I'm sorry, Charysse," she got out before she fled back to Mackenzie's side. She almost collided with Shane in her hurry and haste.

"What's gotten into Candice?" Shane asked. He set his backpack next to Charysse's satchel.

"Big Mac," Marty said. "She was possessed a few weeks ago."

"So are both you guys head over for Char or am I reading the smoke signals wrong?" Bonnie announced, drawing their attention from Candice.

"Well, speaking for myself, I'm fond of Charysse," Marty said. He cast a look at her. "Captivated, actually. Enthralled, even, but definitely not 'head over.' I'm interested in someone else, if you really want to know."

"What about you, Shane?" Bonnie asked. She grinned as she lazily chewed her gum. "Are you seeing anybody?"

Charysse reddened. The other students in the room were busy with schoolwork or socializing, but she still felt that certain ears were waiting along with hers for Shane's answer. It had been almost two weeks since the time they had shared in the greenhouse. They hung together at school, as much as they could, and they'd spoken by phone almost every night. One night, Charysse had been on the phone with him right up to the moment her mother had come home from work at 1 am. Charysse couldn't understand why she was so worried about what Shane would say.

"There's someone," he said. Charysse felt his eyes on her. When she looked up, it was Mackenzie's face she saw. She stared at Charysse with the fixed and piercing gaze of a reptile. "I just haven't worked up the nerve to ask her out," Shane finished.

"Mrs. DiGregorio has inventory at the store on Friday," Bonnie said in a conspiratorial tone. "Why don't you guys come over to Char's and have dinner with us? Charysse makes great lasagna."

"I love lasagna," Marty said. "I'm there."

"What time?" Shane said coolly.

Charysse went from wanting to pinch Bonnie to wanting to hug her.

"Is six too early?" Bonnie asked the small circle.

"Perfect," Marty said. "Can you give me a ride, Shane?"

"Sure," he said.

"Char, is Friday at six good for you?" Bonnie asked.

"It's a date," Charysse said. She looked at Shane. Was it a date? her expression seemed to ask.

"It's a double date," Shane said. He set his hand on the back of Charysse's chair. She sat back, and his hand remained in place. Her hair brushed his hand. When she felt a gentle tug at the back of her head, she knew for sure that she and Shane had just made an official date.

"Give me your hand," Bonnie said to Marty. He presented it to her. She held it, palm up, and used her right index finger to lightly trace numbers in the sensitive center of his palm. By the time she had written all ten digits, Marty's face was flushed and his jaw was clenched tightly. "That's my phone number," she said. "Call me before Friday and I'll tell you what you should bring."

Marty nodded. That was all he was capable of at the moment.

With a loud pop of her gum, Bonnie stood up and pulled her ponytail tight. "Char, where's the ladies'?"

"Down the hall to your right. It's the first door," Charysse said.

"Do I need a pass or anything?" Bonnie asked.

"Nope. Just go."

"I thought you girls liked to go to the bathroom in packs," Shane said.

Charysse liked the soft brush of his fingertips across the back of her shirt. "Bonnie and I aren't like that."

"She's got a way about her," Shane said. "Huh, Marty?"

Marty, his right hand closed as though he were afraid to lose Bonnie's number, smiled as he busily worked on a maze he had started during homeroom that morning. He was oblivious to anything that wasn't Bonnie Gagliardi.

"My Lemke paper is due on Friday," Charysse said to Shane. "It's finished, but I'd like someone to give it a once-over before I give it to him. Would you mind? It's only eight pages. Mackenzie offered, but…"

"Enough said," Shane laughed.

Charysse opened her laptop and called up the document. "I can print it out right now."

Shane moved his desk closer to Charysse's, so close that his outer thigh came into contact with hers. "I can read it right now, off your monitor, if that's okay."

Charysse turned her screen so they could share it. Bonnie returned and winked at Charysse when she saw her hunched close to Shane behind the laptop.

"What are you lookin' at?" Bonnie suddenly demanded as she returned to her seat.

"Yeah, what are you lookin' at?" Marty echoed, sounding exactly like an extra from *The Sopranos*.

"What's the matter?" Charysse asked.

"Stilts over there can't keep her eyes to herself," Bonnie said loud enough for Mackenzie to plainly hear her. "She's lookin' at you like she's in love or something."

"Trust me," Charysse said quietly as she braved another dark look from Mackenzie, "that's definitely more something than love."

Chapter Five

Charysse was on her hands and knees rifling through the pile of books, notebooks and folders on the floor at the base of her locker. Her heart pounded in her ears and throbbed painfully against the cage of her chest as she opened textbooks and violently shook them out.

"Where is it?" she whimpered softly. "I had it this morning. I know I did!"

Charysse didn't notice the quiet footfalls that brought Mackenzie, Bea and Leslie to her side. Candice pulled up the rear, struggling to walk in high-heeled boots while burdened by her own books and Mackenzie's.

"Is something wrong, Charysse?" Mackenzie asked cheerfully.

"Go away!" Charysse snapped. The last thing she needed was Mackenzie's needling.

"Let me think," Mackenzie said, comically tapping her chin with her index finger as though she were deep in serious thought. "I've got it! Dr. Lemke needs his paper today. Is that why you're so stressed out?"

"Why don't you go swallow some mice?" Charysse yelled. "Leave me alone!"

Mackenzie laughed, and it was as clear and light as the chime of a bell. "You lost it, didn't you? That's why you're in such a pissy mood."

Charysse ignored Mackenzie. She stood up and tried to calm herself enough to search her locker one more time from top to bottom. Mackenzie leaned against the locker next to Charysse's. She looked very soft and feminine in a pale pink cashmere dress. She played with a lock of her hair, which she wore loose. "Papers get lost so easily," Mackenzie whispered. "Sometimes you never, ever find them again."

"You took it," Charysse ground out between gritted teeth. "Give it back, or I swear…"

"What?" Mackenzie inquired calmly. "You'll beat me up? You'll get expelled. Colleges don't look favorably upon students who get expelled for assault in their senior year."

"Candice," Charysse began, "do you know where my Lemke paper is? He needs it before the end of school today."

"Come on, ladies," Mackenzie directed as she sauntered away.

"Candice, I know this is supposed to be a joke, but how would you feel if someone broke into your locker and took something you worked really hard on? You know where my paper is. Tell me. Please!"

"Candice!" Mackenzie growled from halfway down the corridor.

Candice's shoulders tightened in her dark blue cashmere sweater. Her eyes closed, displaying the heavy layer of midnight blue shadow coating her eyelids. She took a few steps from Charysse. "She flushed it!" Candice whispered before scurrying after Mackenzie and her crew.

Charysse slumped against the lockers. A frightening wave of nauseating panic rose within her. "What am I going to do?" she asked herself over and over, her hands clasped over her middle. She was still asking herself that when Lotus, Shane and Marty found her there, pale and shaking.

"Mackenzie took my Lemke paper," Charysse told them. "She flushed it."

Lotus put an arm around Charysse, draping her in the billowy sleeve of her ivory peasant blouse. Charysse's chest heaved from the strain of trying not to cry in front of her friends.

"Just print out another copy from your laptop," Marty suggested. He took Charysse's laptop from the pile at her locker, and carried it into the nearest empty classroom. He hooked it up to a printer. "There you go. Crisis averted."

Charysse laughed nervously. "If I'd stayed calm, I would have thought to do this myself. I guess I just got freaked out by Mackenzie's direct assault."

Shane squeezed her shoulder while she searched for her document. "It's not here," she said, her panic planting new roots.

"Look in the recycle bin," Lotus suggested.

Charysse clicked on it. "It's been emptied."

"Where's your backup disc?" Marty asked.

"At home," Charysse said sickly.

"I'll drive you there," Shane said. "We can print it up, no problem."

"Dr. Lemke needs that paper in an hour," Charysse choked over the lump suddenly closing her throat. "He's leaving for the airport right after school. The symposium is tomorrow morning. I don't even have time to print it up and send it to him express mail." Charysse tugged off her jacket and opened an extra button on her shirt. She felt hot and sick. "It wasn't enough for her to punish me. She had to humiliate Dr. Lemke, too." In a sudden burst of anger, Charysse shoved over a desk with her foot. "If she had pulled a stunt like this at Lesterville, she would have ended up bald in the john by the end of the day. How could I have been so stupid? She took the only copy I had here at school."

Shane stepped in before another desk suffered Charysse's wrath. "No, she didn't." He tapped the side of his head. "There's one more."

*

"Charysse, my dear, you don't look well," Dr. Lemke commented after accepting her paper and his original notes.

"I'm just a little worn out," she said.

Dr. Lemke leafed through the pages, glancing at passages here and there. "This is marvelous work, Charysse. I am extremely pleased. You've organized my thoughts well and presented them succinctly. You actually managed to inject a bit of much-needed levity into some of the drier parts. This paper is likely to be published, following the symposium, and I will be honored to share the byline with you."

"Thank you, Dr. Lemke." Charysse mustered as much enthusiasm as she could, considering that all she wanted to do was pull a Norm and jump out of the window.

"Have a lovely weekend, Charysse," Dr. Lemke said. He set the paper in his briefcase, and snapped the briefcase shut. "You've earned it, my dear."

You have no idea, Charysse sighed to herself as she left the room.

Her friends were waiting for her in the corridor. "Well?" Lotus whispered.

"He liked it," Charysse said. "It was fine."

Shane put his arms around her and Charysse went weak against him. She hid her face in his neck, happy to escape Eichorn for a moment. "Thank you so much. You saved me."

She wouldn't have believed it if she hadn't seen him in action herself. He had read her paper once, and four days later he had been able to sit down at a computer and type all eight pages, word for word, from memory. She had printed and proofed each page as he'd typed it in, and she was further amazed when she noticed that he'd corrected two minor typos. And he'd skipped his Western Civilization class to do it.

Marty gave her back a comforting pat. "The day's not over yet," he reminded her. "We still have Lindy's class. I don't know about you, but I'm ready for a showdown. It's about time you had it out with her."

Charysse reluctantly withdrew from Shane. "You're right," she told Marty. She pushed back her hurt and misery to make room for her anger. "It's time to stop this crap once and for all."

*

Charysse rested her head on the wreath of her arms on her desktop. Shane was on one side of her, the warm, comforting weight of his hand between her shoulder blades. Lotus sat on her other side, her normally happy face pinched in a sour look directed at Mackenzie, who had the nerve to approach Shane with a smile on her face.

"You shouldn't have skipped Western Civ.," she told him. "We picked partners for the Cultural Development projects. As luck would have it, you and I ended up together."

Shane's stomach turned. "Donovan?" he called across the room

"Yes?" Donovan looked up from a thick book.

"Who'd you get in Western Civ. today?"

Donovan made a face and jutted his jaw toward Norm, who was furiously rubbing his knuckles along the lengths of his thighs.

"Why are you staring at me?" Norm cried in a sudden panic.

"Trade?" Shane offered Donovan.

"Talk about falling on the sword, man," he chuckled. "Are you sure?"

Shane nodded.

"Then he's all yours." Donovan sat up straighter in his chair and pulled his most disarming smile on Mackenzie. "Looks like it's you and me, Sunshine."

"What's your problem, Shane?" Mackenzie jabbed her fists onto her hips. "You'd rather work with Norm than with me?"

"It's nothing personal, Mackenzie," Shane said. "I'd like to make sure it stays that way."

Mackenzie picked a new target. "What's the matter, Charysse? You look a little sick."

Charysse sat up. She smoothed her hair from her face and took a deep breath. The rest of the class had heard about what Mackenzie had done to Lemke's paper, and the room quieted to witness what would happen next. "I'm fine," Charysse said. "Maybe you've heard that someone broke into my locker, stole a very important paper and flushed it, tampered with my hard drive and basically tried to screw me over. But it all worked out in the end. I got the paper in."

Mackenzie's mouth dropped open, betraying her shock and surprise.

"Dr. Lemke is sharing the byline with me, when he publishes the paper," Charysse said.

"Mac, you only got two acknowledgements last year on Dr. Lemke's papers, right?" Lotus asked.

Mackenzie's face went blood red.

"Miss Cole, are you okay?" Ms. Lindy asked. "Do you need a drink or some fresh air?"

77

"Throw a bucket of water on her," Marty said. "Maybe she'll melt."

Ms. Lindy set down the papers she was grading. "If there's a problem here, the best way to solve it is through communication."

"I agree," Charysse said. "Candice, may I have a word with you?"

"Candice?" Lotus repeated. "You said Mackenzie—"

Marty nudged Lotus, shutting her up.

"Me?" Candice squeaked.

"Let's go outside," Charysse said.

Candice seemed to shrivel as Mackenzie glared at her. "I'd rather stay in here," Candice finally said. "What do you want with me?"

"I want to know what's happened to you," Charysse said, careful not to accuse her directly. There was no rancor in her voice, or even anger. There was only her genuine concern for Candice. "When I first met you in September, you didn't seem like the type who would take part in deliberately hurting someone."

"I'm not." Candice spoke so quietly, it was hard to hear her.

"Then how do you explain what happened with Dr. Lemke's paper?" Charysse insisted.

Candice hugged a notebook to her chest. She stared at her desktop until tears brimmed in her eyes. "I thought things would be different when I came here, but it's exactly the way it was at my old school. There are the popular kids and then there's everyone else. I'm tired of being everyone else. I have friends now, and when they do things, I have to go along with them."

"I was your friend," Charysse said.

"Not like the ones I have now." Candice swiped her face with her hand. "Mackenzie lets me drive her to college parties and she shows me what clothes to buy. She helped me pick out that dress she has on, and the sweater I'm wearing. She shows me how to do my hair and makeup."

"Has she shown you a mirror, Candice?" Lotus burst out. "You look like a Pokémon character!"

"I'm not like you, Charysse!" Candice cried, bolting to her feet. "I'm not this beautiful, exotic, strong person who came in and captured everyone's heart. I'm finally popular, and I won't give it up! I'm sorry about what Mackenzie did to you, but there was no real harm done. You gave Dr. Lemke his paper and everything turned out fine."

"I don't have to stand here and listen to false accusations about me," Mackenzie huffed. She stomped over to her desk and snatched up her magazines and her backpack. "As for you, Candice, you can forget that you ever knew me!"

Mackenzie made a quick escape, leaving Candice alone in the classroom.

"Candice," Ms. Lindy said, "would you like to be excused?"

Candice nodded. Her eyes continued to tear as she gathered her books.

"Candice, I'm sorry," Charysse said. "Do you still have my phone number? In case you want to talk later?"

"No," Candice said dully.

Charysse tore off a corner of notebook paper and wrote her phone number on it. She handed it to Candice.

"I meant, no, that I won't want to talk later," Candice said. "I have to make things right with Mackenzie."

*

Marty held a bouquet of daisies, their long stems limp from the pressure of his hand. He had combed his hair down, parting it on the left side. He wore a plaid, 1950s malt-shop style short coat with brown leather patch pockets. The wide, turned-up cuffs of his jeans revealed blinding white socks and a pair of scuffed brown work boots.

"Good to see you tonight, Shane," Bonnie said after opening the front door and scanning Marty's outfit. "You're handsome as always."

"Thanks, Bonnie," Shane said. He was dressed in a three-quarter length black leather coat, blue jeans, black Doc Marten's and a white shirt.

Marty, none too subtle, cleared his throat and grinned.

"You look handsome, too, Potsie," Bonnie said.

"What's a Potsie?" Marty asked, falling back a step as he and Shane entered Charysse's house.

"Don't they let you geniuses watch *TVLand*?" Bonnie closed the door behind them, and held out her hand for their coats. "Potsie. From that old show, *Happy Days*."

"Oh, yeah," Marty said. He hung his coat on one of the hooks mounted in the foyer. "I wanted to look special tonight."

"I think you pulled it off," Charysse said as she joined them, and invited them into the dining room.

"Is there anything I can do to help?" Shane offered.

Charysse didn't realize that he was speaking. He hadn't dressed up for dinner, but he wasn't wearing his usual school uniform of jeans and sweaters, either. She had grown up with the antique rosewood living room set and the four framed botanical prints on the subtly striped wallpaper, but the energy of Shane's presence gave the room a new, livelier glow.

"Charysse?" Shane said, breaking her out of her reverie.

"Yes? I'm sorry," she began. "I didn't hear what you said."

He smiled and glanced at the table. It was already set for four, along with a colorful garden salad, a cruet of homemade Italian dressing and a dish of freshly grated Parmesan cheese. "It looks like you have everything under control, but is there anything Marty and I can do to help?"

Bonnie set a hand on each boy's shoulder. "Just have a seat and Char and I will bring out the main dish." She took Charysse's hand and the two of them went through a pair of swinging doors and into the hot, brightly lit kitchen.

Charysse slipped on a pair of rose-printed oven mitts. When she opened the oven, the scent of her bubbling lasagna wafted through the room.

"Those guys are in for it tonight," Bonnie said. "Char, your lasagna smells awesome!"

Charysse hefted the big casserole dish out of the oven and onto a large trivet. She had made four times as much as she normally did, just to make sure there would be enough. "Would you take the scali out of the breadmaker? There's a straw basket for it on the counter."

"Char, are you okay?" Bonnie asked. "Your head's been somewhere else since I got here. It wouldn't hurt to crack a smile, you know?"

Charysse set down the fresh basil leaves she was using to garnish the lasagna. "I know. This is my first dinner party and I want everything to be perfect."

Bonnie's smile widened as she daintily arranged the linen cloth beneath the steaming loaf of scali bread. "You really like him, don't you?"

Charysse absently wiped her hands on her skirt as she went to the refrigerator. "Who?" She took a pitcher of iced tea from the top shelf.

"Shane," Bonnie said. "Don't play stupid with me."

"He's been a really good friend to me." Charysse took up a long sprig of fresh mint that had been drying on a paper towel by the sink. She lightly crushed it in her hands before plunging it into the tea.

"He don't look at you like you're just friends," Bonnie said, lowering her voice. "He looks at you like you're made of money and Snickers bars."

"We're just friends. You're the one who invited him here for dinner tonight, not me," Charysse said. She used the tinted glass of the upper oven as a mirror, to make sure there were no spots of pasta sauce or flour on her loose-fitting white sweater. She wore her hair down and she finger combed it from her face. Bonnie joined her, adjusting the neckline of her hot pink sweater so that it revealed more of her shoulders and collarbones.

"You could have said no," Bonnie reminded her.

Charysse turned away, trying to hide her guilty smile. "I didn't want to say no."

"I didn't think so." Bonnie happily popped her gum. "You can thank me later, by helping me study for the Oscar Wilder test I have on Monday. Hey, is he related to Laura Ingalls Wilder?"

*

Stuffed with lasagna, salad and homemade scali, the foursome decided to walk off some of their meal by going to Guiglio's Bakery for dessert. On the way back to Charysse's house, Charysse and Shane moseyed far behind Marty and Bonnie, who chased each other around street lamps and newspaper boxes like puppies.

"You seem a little distracted tonight," Shane said quietly.

Charysse pulled her coat a little closer. The night was mild, for November, but the wind had a bite that penetrated the warmth of her grey wool skirt. "Bonnie said the same thing." They walked on a few more steps before Charysse continued. "I'm having a hard time shaking this afternoon off."

"That's the other thing I wanted to ask you about." Shane drew his left hand from his pocket. As if he had done it hundreds of times before, he took Charysse's right hand. The warmth of his fingers flooded through her, lessening the tension that had been gripping her since Lindy's class. "Why did you go after Candice this afternoon instead of Mackenzie? Everyone knows Mac's the one who took your paper."

"I thought I could help Candice," Charysse said. "I wish she could try just a little more to help herself."

"You're a good person, Charysse. I really am glad that you came to Eichorn. It almost seems like…"

"What?" she asked when he didn't finish.

He stopped, drawing her to him beneath a street lamp. "It almost seems like you're a gift."

She laughed nervously. "I'm just me, Shane. I'm just some chump who happened to luck into Eichorn."

His fingers threaded through her hair, moving it at her temple as he tilted her face up to his. "I've been wanting to kiss you since I first saw you tonight."

Charysse held her breath. Her thoughts began to jumble in her head. She wondered if she had anything stuck between her teeth, or if there was powdered sugar on her chin from the cannolis she had eaten at Guiglio's. She hoped that her breath didn't smell of the roasted garlic she had spread on her bread during dinner, and that, if he kissed her right then and there, that she would be able to kiss him back without it showing that he was only the second boy she had ever kissed.

"Actually, that isn't quite true," he amended with a shy smile. "I've wanted to kiss you since I saw you on the first day of school."

Charysse struggled to find something to do with her hands. She settled on grasping the flaps of his opened jacket. She took in a shuddering breath as his sparkling, blue-green gaze moved over her face. "If I don't ask you now, I might never have the nerve again. May I kiss you, Charysse?"

"Yes," seeped from her parted lips. As if in slow motion, he lowered his head while bringing hers closer. She felt his soft, warm breath on her lips, and she closed her eyes.

"Not on the street, kids," Bonnie said, swooping in to cover Charysse's mouth with her hand. "And not in front of the child."

"Funny," Marty said. "Way to mess up a romantic moment."

"Let's, uh, get back home," Charysse said. She shoved her hands into her pocket and started down the street. "It's getting late. The roughnecks will be out soon. We can play Scrabble or something."

Bonnie linked her arm through Charysse's. The two girls hurried ahead of the boys. "That was close!" Bonnie whispered.

"I know," Charysse said. "Thanks for ruining it for me."

"I didn't mean you," Bonnie said. "Marty grabbed me the second he saw Shane going in for the kill. Marty's been shadowing Shane all night. When Shane laughs, Marty laughs. When Shane held your hand, Marty grabbed my hand. When Shane tried to kiss you, Marty tried to kiss me."

"I thought you liked him."

"I like *Marty*. Not Marty copycatting Shane. We gotta get those two separated."

"Marty's just nervous," Charysse explained. "He likes you a lot. He's working on a maze for you. It looks like a pile of roses."

"Yeah?" Bonnie smiled up at the moon. "He's wicked cool."

"Ask him to show you his maze sometime, the one he works on at home," Charysse advised. "Then you'll see the real Marty."

Bonnie peeked over her shoulder. "He really is amazing, Char."

"So are you, Bon."

"You don't have to say that." Bonnie spat out her gum. "I know I'm not like you and Marty and Shane. This time next year, you guy's will all be at some fancy college and I'll be down at Bunker Hill Community taking candy courses so I can learn to do hair or answer phones at the motor registry."

"Bonnie…" Charysse stopped walking as the boys caught up to them. She didn't know what to say in response to Bonnie's unexpected mood change.

"The only reason Marty came tonight is because he digs you almost as much as Shane does. I don't know why you three geniuses want to hang around with a dummy like me anyway."

"Is that what you think?" Charysse asked her friend. "That I think you're a dummy?"

"No," Bonnie snapped. "Yes! I don't know what I think. If I was as smart as you, I could figure it out."

"Shut up, Bonnie." Marty stood before her, his hands on his hips. "All my life, pretty girls like you avoided me like I was contagious because I was smart. When you invited me to dinner, I thought, 'Thank you, God!' I was finally the guy who got the pretty girl who was also funny and exciting and smart." Marty took a step toward her, which made her stand taller to face him. "Yes, I said smart. Until you said what you just did. Now that was dumb."

Bonnie stared at him as she considered his words. She glanced at Charysse, who recognized the forgiving twinkle in them. Bonnie punched Marty in the arm.

"Ow!" he squawked. "What was that for?"

"That's how us average, public school kids show affection. Or didn't you know that?"

Marty, scowling, leaned forward and gave her a kiss on her cheek.

"What was that for?" Bonnie asked.

"That's how us genius, private school kids show affection."

Bonnie unwrapped a fresh piece of gum. "You like me, Marty?"

"I like you very much."

She grabbed his thumb and gave it a playful tug. "You're smarter than I thought you were."

Bonnie and Marty, walking thumb in hand, turned into Charysse's postage-stamp front yard. Shane waited until they had gone into the house before he took Charysse's hands in his. "When can we do this again?"

"I'm not sure what Bonnie has planned for next weekend, but I'm—"

"You," Shane said. "I meant just you."

"Oh. Ooh."

"Or we can double again, with Marty and Bonnie," he quickly offered.

"No," Charysse said. "Let's give the Kissing Police the night off."

*

Charysse shooed Shane back into the living room to select a board game while she made coffee in the kitchen. She knew that Bonnie would entertain their guests in her absence, but when she heard Bonnie say, "You better be good to her," Charysse stilled and listened.

"Why wouldn't I be?" she heard Shane reply.

"Char's the smartest person I know, but she's real dumb as far as boys go," Bonnie said.

Shane's soft chuckle made Charysse smile as she tucked her thumbnail between her teeth. "I have to say that in this case, Bonnie, she's made a good choice."

"When we was in the tenth grade, Char started goin' out with this guy, Quinn Ludlow," Bonnie began. That name made Charysse's skin break out in unpleasant goose bumps. "Quinn was a senior, and, oh my god, he was drop dead and slap your mama gorgeous. He looked like Brad Pitt, but younger and with better hair. Swear to God."

Charysse pictured Bonnie with her right hand raised, then genuflecting because of the swear.

"Quinn's father had an auto body shop, so he always had a flash car and money in his pocket," Bonnie went on. "He was like, *king* of Lesterville. He dated all the cheerleaders and this one girl at Scarbury High who used to do modeling in Boston all the time. When he asked Char out, I said, 'Char, he's just usin' you to get a passin' grade in Senior Algebra.' Senior Algebra is like, totally remedial. It's ninth grade algebra but for seniors, which should tell you just how dumb Quinn was. But Char wouldn't listen."

Charysse went back to the coffeemaker. She arranged four cups in a line and busied herself with opening the bag of anisette cookies she had purchased at Guiglio's, but she could still plainly hear Bonnie.

"I guess she was in love," Bonnie said. "He was her first boyfriend and he took her out places and to parties and stuff. He brought her flowers on their study dates. He was a real player."

"What went wrong?" Shane asked.

Bonnie's voice rose in anger. "The minute he got his winter report card, he dumped her." She snapped her fingers. "Like that. All he wanted was a B in math. He wanted to apply to Morgan Technical College early admissions, and he needed at least a B in math. But MoCo pulled the rug from under Quinn. The B wasn't enough. MoCo wanted to see if he could keep his grades up in Spring, too. So what does he do? He calls Char and goes, 'I'm sorry, forgive me, I need you, I was *baaaaad*!'"

Charysse smothered a sad laugh in her hand. Bonnie's impersonation of Quinn's toneless, nasal voice always cracked her up, even after the pain he had caused her.

"He only wanted her to tutor her through Spring, and my genius friend bought his Poor Pitiful Me routine," Bonnie said. "I was wicked pissed."

"She went back to him?" Marty asked.

"That's what I thought, too, but Char was two steps ahead," Bonnie said.

"What did she do?" Shane asked.

"She told him that she would help him, and so he starts giving her the treatment—candy, flowers, stuffed animals. You know. She throws it all away, right, except for some of the candy. I was glad to take some of it off her hands for her. I love chocolate like I love air! So anyways, his first algebra test in January comes along, and it couldn't be easier, even for a dumb bum like Quinn. It was a take home test! All he had to do was look in his book for the formulas and stuff. So he comes over and sits right here on this sofa, and he's watchin' a videotape of Star Wars while girlfriend does his test for him. I was here and I was so made at her, I went home.

"Quinn turns in the test and the next morning, he gets called into the principal's office," Bonnie said. "It seems that his test answers were correct, but they'd all been written in Greek numbers. Seriously. The teacher knew that Char had done Quinn's test. She got a week's detention for taking the test for him, and Quinn got suspended."

"Did the suspension ruin his chances at MoCo?" Marty asked.

"No," Bonnie said, "but he thought it did. He came stormin' over here and kicked in the door when Char wouldn't let him in. Her mom was at work, so she was here all alone."

"What a headcase," Marty said. "Was Charysse alright?"

"I guess so," Bonnie answered. "She never talked about it. The cops came and everything, and Quinn was arrested. His dad got a lawyer who arranged for Quinn to get probation, and you know what else? He got into MoCo. He's there now, probably majoring in Nose Picking. Char hasn't dated anyone since."

Charysse was leaning back on the white counter, her head down, when Shane entered the kitchen. She wasn't aware of him until she felt his finger graze her forehead as he brushed a lock of hair from her face.

"Coffee's cold." He nodded toward the four mugs that no longer steamed.

"Yep. Bonnie's tales run long."

"She's a good storyteller. She's like the tribal historian of Lesterville High."

Charysse turned to dump the contents of the mugs into the sink. "I'll pour fresh coffee."

Shane stopped her with a gentle hand on her shoulder. "Did he hurt you?"

Shane was such a nice guy, and he was everything Quinn wasn't. His tender inquiry touched Charysse's heart in an unexpected way. His concern made her feel safe. The feeling was so nice, it brought hot tears to her eyes. She shook her head as she tried to back away from him. He cupped her face, his grip firm but gentle as he guided her gaze to his. "Did he hurt you?"

His caring made it impossible for her to push back the tears. She blinked, sending fat tears to leave cool trails down her cheeks. "He scared me, that's all." It was painful for her to speak over the lump wedged in her throat. "I thought he'd at least look at his stupid test before he handed it in. It all just got out of hand."

He searched her eyes as if trying to divine an unspoken secret. Charysse hung her fingers loosely over his wrists. His gaze moved from her eyes to her lips as he moved closer and wrapped her in his arms. The thud of his heart within the secure wall of his embrace was just what she needed after the day she had had and Bonnie's recollection of the incident with Quinn. Her arms went around him, and she hooked her hands over his broad shoulders. She exhaled, and the quiet breath seemed to issue from the soles of her feet.

Chapter Six

Ms. Lindy casually strolled among the students, glancing at their work or briefly participating in their conversations. She paused at Marty's desk. He sat up, showing her the paper he had been hunched over so intently.

"That's a nice one," she said, smiling at Marty's maze of interlocking long-stemmed roses. "Who?"

"Her name is Bonnie," Marty said proudly. "She's a civilian."

"She's a moron," Mackenzie interjected. "A-Mazing here has dipped his toes in the lukewarm waters of the Lesterville genetic pool."

Marty returned to his maze, shaking his head. He tried to focus his attention on his work, but the point of his micro-tip pen bent under the pressure he unknowingly applied to it. Two desks away from him, Charysse looked at Ms. Lindy, wondering if the teacher would do anything to diffuse the explosion she saw building behind Marty's clenched jaw.

"You're meaner than a rattlesnake, Mackenzie!" Marty shouted, rising to his feet. "Why do you have to be so damned snobby?"

The quiet room went silent. Ms. Lindy's black loafers made no sound as she returned to her desk.

"It just bothers me to see a cute, unquestionably brilliant guy like you dating down." Mackenzie answered Marty's question, but she looked at Shane the whole time. "What would your kids be like?"

"Kids?" Marty laughed bitterly. "Are you high? I'm not thinking about kids or marriage. I'm just glad to get a date! At my old school, girls treated me like I was some kind of circus geek. They'd only talk to me to ask me to hide their names in a maze, or to race their calculators doing math problems. And the guys ... I should have beat myself up before I left the house most days, to save them the trouble. Being smart is not an entitlement or a blessing. It's luck most days, and a curse when it comes to girls." Marty sat down and leaned back in his chair. His tone softened when he said, "Except for Bonnie. She treats me like I'm a regular guy. I'll take a Lesterville girl over a witch like you any day, Mackenzie."

Donovan's quiet laughter broke the silence.

"Are you going to let him call me names right here in your class, Ms. Lindy?" Mackenzie almost shrieked.

"This is our class, Miss Cole, and I believe you established the precedent of name-calling by referring to Marty's friend as a moron," Ms. Lindy said.

Mackenzie gritted her pearly little teeth in a grimace. She held the sides of desk so tight, her knuckles went as white as her suede boots. Candice, sitting next to Mackenzie, squinted her eyes shut as though Mackenzie would turn on her.

"Take cover," Lotus whispered to Charysse, "I think her head's going to explode."

"Stay out of this, Lotus!" Mackenzie shouted.

"Is something bothering you, Mackenzie?" Chrysanthemum delivered her question in a low, calm voice that only further aggravated Mackenzie. "I sense a little misplaced aggression."

"Misplaced aggression?" Bradley repeated. "Is that what you gals are calling PMS these days?"

"Shut up, Bradley," Lotus and Chrysanthemum said.

"What?" Bradley asked innocently. "We're all adults here."

"Chrys is right," Donovan said. "What's the deal, Mac? Do you genuinely care whom Marty hangs with?"

"Of course not," she spat. She made a production of straightening her black silk blouse.

"Methinks she doth protest too much," Shane said. He leaned closer to Charysse, to whisper, "Maybe Big Mac's got the hots for A-Mazing."

Charysse chuckled. "That would truly be amazing," she said under her breath.

"So you're against me now, too, Shane?" Mackenzie accused, her flashing eyes wide in a curious mix of anger and hurt.

Shane sighed wearily. "I'm not against anyone, and you know it."

"We go back a long way," Mackenzie said. The wrath had left her voice, replaced by a tenderness none of her classmates had ever heard. "We've been a part of each other's lives since kindergarten. That's a lot of history."

Shane said nothing. He moved the tip of his pencil lazily across the "S" on the cover of his Physics book. Charysse opened her French book and began reading a story about Louis Pasteur.

"My dad just bought a new Porsche," Mackenzie said. She elegantly crossed one long leg over the other. "Why don't you stop by this afternoon and see it?"

"Thanks, but I have plans," Shane said. "I have to study for my French exam."

"Maybe Saturday then," Mackenzie said. "I'll tell my dad that you're coming. He'll leave the keys for us."

"Can't," Shane said, snapping his fingers in mock regret. "I have a study date."

"With...?" Mackenzie's eyes darkened.

"You don't know her."

Mackenzie straightened up in her chair. Charysse slumped further into hers. "Really?" Mackenzie said, drawing the word out. "For some reason, I thought that you and...Charysse...had a thing."

"We do," Shane said, sending hot blood to Charysse's cheeks.

"You said I didn't know her," Mackenzie sputtered.

"That's just it," Shane said. "You don't."

*

Shane's books and notes were spread out on the dark green plaid of the worn sofa while Charysse worked at a big teak desk. They had eaten leftover Chinese food for dinner, and their plates were stacked on the low coffee table in front of the sofa. Charysse looked up from her work to see Shane standing at the bookcase that lined one of the walls. His fingertips moved along the spines of some of the thick, leather-bound volumes. He picked up a wooden decoy of a mallard and brought it to the desk.

"Quack," he said with a smile that cleared Charysse's head of the verb conjugations she'd been studying.

Shane reached for the humidor at the end of the desk. When he started to open it, Charysse leaped from her leather swivel chair and snatched it from him. "I'm sorry," she hastily apologized. She tucked the humidor under her arm as she joined him at the front of the desk. "These are my dad's. *Were* my dad's," she corrected. She opened the lid of the burled cherrywood box and took a deep whiff of the cigars within it. "They're starting to lose their scent."

"Where is your dad?" Shane asked. "You never talk about him."

"St. Patrick's," she said. "Plot 268. He's beneath a gorgeous oak."

"How did it happen?" Shane took the humidor and closed it. He set it on the desk. Charysse sat on the edge of the desk while Shane took a seat near her, on the sofa.

"He was at a softball game. Lesterville versus Everett, Adult Summer League. He got hit in the chest with a hard line drive. It knocked the wind out of him, but he was able to finish the game. He came home, had dinner, and he and mom and I watched a movie. *The Dirty Dozen*. He loved war pictures. He kissed me goodnight before I went to bed. I woke up the next morning to my mother's screams."

Charysse wandered about the study, noticing how little it had changed since her father's death. The subdued track lighting aimed at the bookcase hid the fact that most of the items in the room hadn't been touched in a long time. Christopher DiGregorio's books were where he had left them. Most of the papers in his desk hadn't been touched, neither by Charysse nor her mother. A few of Charysse's things had found their way into the room—her spelling bee ribbon hung around the neck of her father's golfing trophy, a pair of her shoes sat under a lamp table by the door, a few of her magazines were piled on an end table flanking the sofa—but for the most part, the study still belonged to her father.

"He died in his sleep," she said. "The coroner said that the sac around my dad's heart had been bruised, and that it had filled with blood as he slept. It killed him. It was peaceful and painless and…sudden."

"That's better than going slowly, one day at a time for years," Shane said.

"He was thirty-four years old. He's supposed to be *here*."

"Is that why you keep this room?"

"I feel closer to him here. When I was little, I used to sleep on that sofa while he was working."

"You were twelve when he died," Shane remarked.

"How did you know?"

Shane pointed to a calendar mounted on the wall near the desk. It was six years old.

"It seems like it's been longer than that," Charysse said. "I can't remember the way his laugh sounded, or how he liked his eggs. I wish I'd noticed more about him. That's why I like the humidor. He used to smoke one of those cigars every Fourth of July, while he worked the grill. The scent reminds me so much of him."

"What did he do for a living?" Shane asked.

"He was a psychologist. He was a very good therapist."

"Like father, like daughter," Shane said.

"I miss him."

"Losing a parent is harder than people realize."

Charysse recalled what Marty had once told her, about Shane's mother having been sick. "You lost your mom?"

Shane looked at her, the bare emotion in his face drawing her to his side. "I think so."

*

"Thanks for coming out here on such short notice," Shane said as he let Charysse into his house. "My Western Civ. project is due tomorrow, and Norm just bailed on me."

"What did you do to him?" Charysse took off her jacket. Shane took it and slung it over the back of the sofa as they passed through his spacious living room and into the airy kitchen. Charysse's eyes popped. "Maybe I should run, too."

"It looks worse than it is." Shane went to the stove, where the contents of two pots steamed and hissed.

Charysse stared at the cabbages, spinach leaves, phyllo dough and raw ground beef haphazardly stacked on the counter nearest the sink. The central prep counter held a big container of opened feta cheese, a gigantic jar of kalamata olives, a block of yellow cheddar cheese, jars of anise seeds, cumin seeds, pine nuts, walnuts and a tub of dates. At least five cookbooks were opened to various recipes, and rows of things that looked like charcoal briquettes lined two cookie sheets that steamed on wire racks on another counter. Footprints in the flour sprinkled on the tile floor told the story of Norm's presence and departure, as did a handprint on the counter that looked and smelled like honey.

The faint bleat of an animal drew Charysse to the wide, arched window above the sink. There on the McKenna's deck, tied to the leg of a picnic table, was a lamb.

"Norm's contribution," Shane said, handing Charysse an apron. "Our assignment is to prepare a feast fit for an ancient Greek nobleman. I opened the feta cheese, Norm spooked, and he booked outta here. I don't think he'll be back. Could you help me out?"

"When is your project due?"

Shane smiled nervously. "Tomorrow, by sixth period. Everyone in Western Civ. is supposed to skip lunch and eat a Greek feast. A bunch of us combined our projects, and the banquet will tie them all together."

"Sounds like fun." Charysse slipped the apron over her neck. Shane tied the strings in a bow at the small of her back.

"Maybe I should have stuck with Mackenzie," Shane said.

"Do you know what project she chose?" Charysse asked.

"Does it matter?"

"She got Courtship, Mating and Marriage. Would you rather be doing that with her, than this?"

Shane surveyed his messy kitchen and the lamb scampering across his deck. When his gaze returned to Charysse, he said, "Absolutely not."

Shane kept reminding her that it was his project. Even so, she took charge. She cleaned up the flour and wiped down the counters while Shane wrote down the menu and organized the ingredients for each dish. Starting with the most time-consuming dishes first, Charysse created a game plan and divided the cooking tasks between them.

"How do you know so much about cooking?" Shane asked as he watched her make small patties from a mixture of ground beef, pine nuts and green peppercorns.

"My Grandma Rosina," Charysse said. "When my mother went back to work, she moved in with us. Every night I would help her cook dinner and on Sundays and holidays, she would make these huge Italian feasts. Every Christmas Eve we would do calamari and lobster and scallops and mussels, and on Christmas Day, it was lasagna and brijoles."

"What are brijoles?" Shane, no slouch in the kitchen himself, rolled a mixture of rice and spices in grape leaves.

"Brijoles are steak stuffed with prosciutto or bacon, cheese, spinach and spices all tied up with string and simmered for hours in gravy. Well, that's what we Italians call red sauce. They're so good."

"I'm thinking I'll be paying you and Grandma Rosina a visit this Christmas," Shane said. "Will you be helping her prepare a big family dinner for Thanksgiving on Thursday?"

"She died when I was sixteen," Charysse said. "Mom and I are going to Bonnie's for Thanksgiving. They always do a big dinner. Last year, there were twenty-two people. She's already invited Marty. I'm sure Bonnie would love for you to come, if you want. Bring your mom and dad, too."

"That reminds me." Shane stole a look at the big aluminum clock mounted above the window. "I'll be right back."

He left the kitchen and retreated down a short corridor. With the Greek hamburgers ready for the oven, Charysse washed her hands at the sink and closed the cookbooks. She was using plastic wrap to cover a batch of Must Rolls when soft voices reached her ears. The voices became progressively louder, and she couldn't avoid overhearing what was said.

"Mom," Shane said in a soft but insistent voice, "you have to take them. Come on, now."

"No," came a muffled, sleepy female voice. "Leave me alone. I want to sleep."

"It's time for your meds," Shane said. "Do you want me to call the doctor?"

"Go away," the voice said, the rest of the words too muffled for Charysse to make out.

"I'll go just as soon as you take your pills."

Charysse turned on the water in the sink, to drown out any further conversation. Shane never spoke of his mother. He rarely ever spoke of his father, who was an economics professor at Tufts University. When Charysse heard footsteps enter the kitchen, she shut off the water and turned around.

"Hello," said a man in a wool coat as he set a briefcase on the seat of a chair in the breakfast nook.

The man was a stranger, but he wasn't strange at all to Charysse. His wavy dark hair was starting to go a bit silver at his temples, but it was every bit as thick as Shane's. His skin was pale, the famed "Scottish blue," she'd once heard a comedian joke. Shane's skin was more olive and tanned, a characteristic likely inherited from his Italian mother. The man approached Charysse, his hand outstretched, and she recognized the familiar deep blue of his smiling eyes.

"You must be Mr. McKenna," Charysse said, wiping her wet hands on her apron. She shook the hand he offered. "I'm—"

"Charysse," he finished, pronouncing her name correctly through a Scottish accent far more distinct than Shane's. "My son has told me quite a lot about you."

"Only the good things are true," she chuckled.

"My goodness." Geoff McKenna surveyed the kitchen. "Shane told me that you were a good cook, but this…this defies description." He bent slightly, to catch the aroma of one of the Greek desserts. "May I?"

"Please," Charysse said. She handed him a napkin.

Mr. McKenna took one of the tiny bundles and popped it into his mouth. "Interesting," he mumbled around the tidbit. "This is delicious. What is it?"

"Aliter Dulcia," Charysse said. "The Ancient Greeks served it with wine and perfume between courses during dinner. It's made of ground walnuts and pine nuts, honey, milk, eggs, ground pepper and a few other things you'd probably rather not know about."

Out in the darkness on the deck, the lamb bleated, catching Mr. McKenna's attention. "Is that what I think it is?"

"Yes. And I had nothing to do with it. I'm strictly kitchen help. Farm animals aren't my thing."

"It appears that Dr. Pendergast's Western Civ. will be the place to be tomorrow," Mr. McKenna said. "These dishes look wonderful."

"I hope they taste wonderful, too," Charysse said. "Shane worked really hard on this."

Mr. McKenna went to the towel rack mounted on the wall above the sink. He wet it, wrung it out, and handed it to Charysse. "You have flour on your forehead and honey on your shirt front," he said. "My son isn't the only one who's been working hard. Speaking of my offspring, where is he?"

"Here, Dad," Shane said. He stepped into the kitchen with an empty water glass in one hand. He set it in the sink.

"How were things this afternoon?" Mr. McKenna asked as he took off his jacket.

Charysse was only mildly surprised to see that Mr. McKenna was wearing jeans and a sweater. The family resemblance included their wardrobes.

"Good," Shane answered. "Can Charysse stay for dinner?"

"It's nothing fancy," Mr. McKenna said. "I was planning to order in pizza."

"Can you stay?" Shane asked her.

"Sure," she said. "I have the car tonight."

"Will you two excuse me?" Mr. McKenna said just before he left the kitchen. "I haven't said hello to your mother."

"I'll call in the pizza," Shane said. He pulled a stack of menus from a basket on the top of the refrigerator. He sorted through them before he settled on Greg's Roast Beef and Pizza. Charysse gazed about the kitchen while Shane placed the order with someone with whom he seemed to be on very friendly terms.

Charysse liked Shane's kitchen. White eyelet curtains covered the lower half of the large windows. The countertops, the ones they hadn't used, were spotless. Small appliances and canisters of coffee, tea, pasta and cookies were arranged neatly against the cheery tile border affixed to the wall. Recessed lighting above the sink and the central prep station cast a warm glow on the covered trays and platters of food that Shane would have to transport to Eichorn. It was a well-ordered and efficient kitchen, designed and stocked by someone who enjoyed being in it. Charysse became more and more curious about who that someone could be.

*

"Is your mom okay?" Charysse asked quietly as Shane walked her out to her car. He slowed his pace, then stopped altogether. He shoved one hand in his pocket and clapped the other one against the back of his head. "I'm sorry, it's none of my business," she said.

Dinner had been a fun yet peculiar affair. Between telling jokes and funny stories about Shane's Scottish grandparents, the father and son took turns excusing themselves from the table to check on the one member of the family who actually had everyone's attention: Shane's mother. Charysse, her curiosity getting the better of her, had positioned herself at the kitchen table so that she could see down the corridor and into the room the two McKennas kept visiting. Armed with her observations, she had taken a chance and asked Shane about his mother.

"It's okay," he said. "You've probably heard all kinds of things at school about my mother. The kids talk about her like she's Boo Radley."

"She was watching us," Charysse said.

Shane's eyes became as wide and bright as the full moon.

"I saw her," Charysse continued. "She cracked the door and watched us nearly the whole night."

"That's not possible," Shane said. He walked a step ahead of Charysse, further from his well-lit Colonial. "She's on medication. The pills knock her out. The cat must have nudged the door open."

"She must be pocketing her pills because she was at the door, watching us have dinner and clean up." Charysse caught a movement in her peripheral vision, but she didn't turn around for a better look. She took Shane's sleeve and pulled him close to her side. "Take a peek at her window when you go back into the house. She's watching us right now."

"Dad's probably in there," Shane said. "It's past his bed time."

They stood at the curb, leaning against the middle-aged Camry Charysse shared with her mother. "Want to hear something funny?" Shane asked. "I almost transferred out of Eichorn over the summer. I was offered a place in the freshman class at MIT for this fall."

"Why didn't you take it?" Charysse inwardly thanked God and all his angels that Shane hadn't taken it.

Shane smiled and stared at his feet. "I wanted to have the whole senior year experience. It's not the same at Eichorn as it is at other schools since we don't have Homecoming or winter formals or things like that, but I wanted to stay there. I had the feeling that there would be something different, something special about this year."

"Every girl at school has a crush on you, Shane." Charysse tucked locks of her hair behind her ears. "Any one of them would have killed to make this year special for you."

"I don't want any other girl. I want you."

Since when did it get so hot at night in November? Charysse wondered. She swiped her hand across her brow, which was suddenly beading with perspiration. She had hoped that they would get the chance to finish what Bonnie had interrupted on their double date last week, but the moment snuck up on her. Why did I have onions on my pizza? she moaned to herself. "Are you going to kiss me now?" she blurted.

"The thought had crossed my mind." He smiled softly.

A glint of light from a downstairs window in Shane's house captured Charysse's attention. "See!" she whispered. "Your mom's watching us right now."

Shane looked at the house. "There's nothing…" He turned back to Charysse, his disbelief plain on his face. "At first I thought it was my dad, but—"

"Your dad doesn't wear a diamond ring on his left hand," Charysse said.

"Mom must be ditching her pills," he said. "Why would she do that?"

"Because she doesn't really need them."

"Yes, she does. She suffers from clinical depression. It started a few years ago, when…when my sister died."

Charysse took his hand and cupped his face, giving in to her instinct to comfort. "Shane, I'm so sorry."

"I was thirteen when Marlys was born. She was a surprise, but a welcome one. Mom always wanted more children, but it just never happened. Marlys had a congenital heart defect and she died two days after she was born. The doctors hadn't expected her to last as long as she did. Mom hasn't been the same since. She wrote *Song For My Children* a few months after Marlys died. The book was supposed to be her way of getting her grief out, and I suppose it did. But once she didn't have her grief, she didn't have anything."

"What about you?"

"Me?"

"How did you handle your sister's death?"

He shrugged a shoulder. He wouldn't meet Charysse's eyes. "I got sent to my grandparents' house. Marlys never came home from the hospital. I never saw her. I've never even seen a picture of her."

"You knew that she was alive," Charysse said. "You knew that you had a sister."

Charysse bit the inside of her lip to stave off tears. The McKenna house looked like something from a Hallmark holiday card, but right then Charysse knew that looks were truly deceiving. "Your mom is a lost soul. So are you."

"How so?"

"Your mom is depressed, but she doesn't need pills. She needs to come through to the other side, but she's stuck in the abyss."

"What abyss?"

"Sadness. Hopelessness. Despair. You're going to have to yank her through it, instead of feeding her pills."

"Dad and I do everything to help her," Shane said defensively. "Dad's whole teaching schedule and my school schedule revolve around her. She never liked any of the nurses that Dad hired for her, so we take care of her. She's always worse around the holidays. She'll be better in January, after New Year's."

"When was the last time the three of you went on a family vacation? When was the last time you and your dad went to a movie together?"

"Not since before the baby died."

"I'll mom-sit for you," Charysse decided.

"It's not that simple," Shane sighed.

"Sure it is. Bonnie's uncle's mechanic offered us tickets to the Patriots on Thanksgiving Sunday. They're yours. You and your dad can go to the Pats. It should be a good game, and the stadium is incredible."

Shane stood there staring at her, his surprise, appreciation and amazement playing over his handsome features. "You're incredible. You know I can't say no to Pats tickets."

"And they're reeaally good seats," she cooed.

"If my mom wasn't watching us right now, I'd kiss you," he said.

"So you'll take the tickets?"

"You betcha." He stroked Charysse's hair. "Now all I have to do is spend the next ninety-six hours convincing my dad."

*

"Mel Gibson, eat your heart out," Lotus whispered under her breath when Shane entered their Western Civilization class dressed as a Greek warrior. "I haven't seen a Scot look this good in a skirt since I saw *Braveheart*."

Shane was part of Lotus's project—Ancient Greek Fashion and Cosmetology. To present her project, Lotus—who was dressed as a handmaiden in a loose, sleeveless tunic and skirt trimmed in wide green and gold braid—had costumed several members of the class as well as a few friends she had enlisted. Charysse was one of them, in the reluctant role of Lotus's warrior's wife.

"I haven't dressed up like this since my fifth-grade Halloween party," Charysse whispered through a self-conscious smile as Shane, covering her hand with his as she clutched his forearm, led her into the classroom-turned-Ancient-Greek-courtyard. Chrysanthemum, wearing a costume identical to her sister's, proceeded before Charysse and Shane, sprinkling rose petals in their path.

Dr. Pendergast, in the flowing robes of a Greek aristocrat, sat at the head of a plywood table painted to look like stone. The students in his class lined the long sides of the table. Donovan and Mackenzie had made half-hearted attempts to dress in costume by draping white bed sheets about their bodies. Candice, dressed in a simple belted tunic, stood near a wall behind the table, in the role of a servant girl.

Shane sat Charysse on a chair draped in dark blue velvet. The rich coloring of the fabric made her pale gold robes even more vibrant. Lotus had styled Charysse's long hair in an intricate bundle of braids secured by a gold foil headdress that looked like a priceless Grecian artifact. Along with the headdress, Lotus had made a pair of gold foil bands for Charysse's wrists and a pair of earrings accented with glass painted to look like amber. Spiraling tendrils of Charysse's hair caressed the elegant length of her neck exposed by her gown, which was trimmed with gold braid.

Bradley wore jute sandals that nicely matched the robe belting his shoulder-baring squire's costume. He stood at the ready to take the red cloak Shane removed from his shoulders with a flourish, revealing the armored breastplate Lotus had made from a latex cast of Shane's chest. Bradley, who already carried Shane's sword and shield, took the cloak and backed away with exaggerated humility to his "master."

"My, my," Dr. Pendergast said. He stroked his chin. His dark eyes twinkled beneath his silvery-white hair. "When you students decide to do a project, you really do a project."

"We decided that our presentations would be most effective if we combined them," Shane said, speaking as the group's general. "Candice's group did Architecture and Furniture, and they constructed the 'courtyard' and the table here. Bradley's group did Manners and Society, Lotus, as you can see, did an awesome job with the costumes for her Fashion and Cosmetology, and Norm and I prepared the food for our part."

Norm, in exchange for having bagged out during the cooking of the banquet, had agreed to dress as a lower slave. He wore his belted, sleeveless tunic over his usual costume of black pants and shirt. All of the food had been stored and reheated in the cafeteria, and Norm had managed to transport it all to Dr. Pendergast's class without dropping any of it. Norman and Bradley's group served everyone before sitting down to plates of their own.

Before he started eating, Shane took off his helmet and handed it to Bradley, who giggled when the bristles of the brushy crest topping the helmet tickled him under his chin.

During the meal, Dr. Pendergast and the students freely asked questions of the students who had made their presentations. Dr. Pendergast was impressed with everyone's hard work, but he made particular note of the food. "Mr. McKenna, I had no idea you were such a good chef. Truthfully, I had no idea what to expect this afternoon, but this meal is spectacular. Those Greek hamburgers, the isicia omentata you spoke of, were delicious and the Must Rolls were heavenly."

"I called in some reinforcements, Dr. Pendergast," Shane admitted. "I couldn't have done this alone." Beneath the table, Shane gave Charysse's hand a gentle squeeze.

"Wise men know their limitations." Dr. Pendergast's nut-brown cheek was stuffed with meatballs. "Crandall?" he called to the other end of the table. "Aren't you going to eat?"

"I *am* eating," said Crandall Fried, the closest thing Eichorn had to a bonafide mad scientist. Crandall, who looked 21st-century normal in a green turtleneck, a Shetland wool sweater and dark khaki corduroy trousers, shifted his wily blue eyes toward his plate. Sitting there on the bare white ceramic disk was a pair of cubes an inch high.

"By the Gods, Crandall," Dr. Pendergast improvised, "can't you leave off the F-Cubes for one afternoon?"

"I'm the first human trial," Crandall argued. He flipped a long lock of his sandy hair from his forehead. "I'm on Day 77, and as you can see, my F-Cube is living up to the hype. I can't eat anything else yet."

Charysse squinted, trying to see the F-Cubes she had heard about. Crandall had already invented a fat substitute that had been purchased for millions by a Japanese food company. Crandall's latest adventure in non-nutritive nutrition was the F-Cube—the F^3—Crandall's Food-Free Food. Charysse had never spoken to Crandall about his project, nor had she ever sampled one herself. But seeing the thing for the first time, she trusted the assessments Marty and Lotus had given her: that the F-Cube looked like tofu, had the texture of an eraser, and tasted like the inside of an old sneaker.

"Pardon me, Crandall," Charysse began graciously in keeping with her role as a warrior's wife, "may I ask a personal question of you?"

Crandall's lean face broke in a happy smile that revealed the slight grayish discoloration of his teeth—a side effect of the F^3. "Yes. I would be honored to be the subject of your kind attention."

"Are you actually living on your F-Cubes?" Charysse asked. "You don't eat anything else?"

"Six F-Cubes three times a day, plus a vitamin and mineral supplement," Crandall said. "I've lost 20.8 pounds since the beginning of my human trial."

No wonder his clothes look so baggy, Charysse thought. Crandall was practically a stick figure before he began his trial.

"If the F-Cube has no food, how is it that they're keeping you alive?" Charysse asked. Students quieted their eating and chatting to listen.

"Everything in the cube is synthesized," Crandall said. "All the fat, carbohydrates and proteins are balanced according to the caloric needs of the average, 18-year-old American male with a moderately fit lifestyle. As soon as I finish my 90-day trial, I'll be ready to present the product to the Food and Drug Administration. After that, it's 'Hello, World!' from my F-Cube. I've already figured out an ad slogan." Crandall shoved one of the cubes onto the tip of his middle finger. He thrust it at his classmates. "'When someone says 'F' you…it's a good thing.'"

"By the Gods," Dr. Pendergast said.

"Forgive me, for spoiling your marketing plans, Crandall," Charysse said, " but 'It's a good thing' is already taken. That phrase is associated with Martha Stewart."

"Hmm," Crandall said, plucking the bland block from his finger. "I guess I'll just stick with 'F' You. Thanks for the heads up."

"I have something for you, Shane," Mackenzie said as she left her place beside Donovan.

"Timeo Danaoset dona ferentes," Charysse muttered under her breath.

Shane looked at her, a tiny smile on his face. "'I fear Greeks even bearing gifts,'" he translated, watching Mackenzie approach him. "You and me both, Charysse."

Mackenzie stood next to Shane, sizing him up in his warrior's gear. "This a little friendly suggestion, but don't you think you could have found someone who's actually in the class to dress up with you? I would have gladly been the warrior's wife."

"When Lotus and I asked you if you and Donovan wanted to present your project with the rest of us, you said no," Shane said.

"And I asked Charysse to wear that costume," Lotus said. "I was going to wear it myself, but when she tried it on for me so I could hem it, I decided that it looked best on her."

"You really do look beautiful, Charysse," Donovan said with a teasing flash of his brown eyes.

Donovan gave her the look that had captured or broken the hearts of every girl in school that wasn't already lost to Shane. Charysse was immune to his flirtations. Shane's gaze told her the same thing Donovan had in words, but Shane's was the one opinion that mattered to her.

Mackenzie complained as she went back to her seat. "Dr. Pendergast, I don't think it's fair that practically anyone can just barge in on our class."

"Miss Cole," Bradley began auspiciously, "if this were truly an Ancient Greek household, the man of the house would have ordered me to drag you outside and have you beaten for insulting his wife. The Greeks placed great importance on hospitality. The only thing worse than not offering a guest practically everything within the walls of your home, was when a guest turned on her host. Especially a female guest. If Charysse wanted to, she could demand that you serve as her slave for insulting her. Of course, with you being from Sparta, we should have expected you to behave this way in the home of a respected warrior of Athens."

"This isn't Ancient Athens, you hormonally-challenged little gnome," Mackenzie spat.

"Until the bell rings, it is," Dr. Pendergast said. "Shane, how do you wish to handle this ill-mannered guest of yours?"

"I don't think a beating would do her any good," Shane said thoughtfully.

"She'd like it if it came from you," Donovan leered.

Shane braced a bare forearm on the table and turned to Charysse. "Meli, what do you want to do with this unpleasant guest?"

Charysse shook her head slightly in confusion. He'd called her 'meli' ... the word was familiar, but she couldn't place where she'd seen it or what it meant.

"Begging your pardon, Shane," Bradley said, "but as the man of the house, it's up to you to determine the punishment for this miscreant." He tugged on the sleeve of Mackenzie's knit top. She violently snatched her arm away.

"Are you seriously going to let them keep humiliating me this way, Dr. Pendergast?" Mackenzie almost shrieked. "This is supposed to be a game, not a public forum to bash Mackenzie Cole."

Dr. Pendergast's jaw tightened. "I don't view this assignment as a 'game,' Miss Cole," he said. His calm tone belied his rising temper. "Although clearly you do, and I'll be sure to take that into consideration when I'm calculating your grade."

"Donovan and I presented our project on Monday," Mackenzie protested. "None of this stuff today has anything to do with it."

"Certainly it does," the teacher said. "You and Donovan taught us all about Courtship, Mating and Marriage in Ancient Greece. Had you learned your own lesson, you would have known what you were getting yourself into the second you decided to leave your seat and insult the wife of your host, a respected warrior of Athens."

Hectic spots of red appeared in Mackenzie's cheeks, as though she suddenly had hives. Her shoulders rose and fell with the deep, quick breaths as she swallowed her anger and frustration. "Anything I say will just make this worse!"

Charysse bowed her head. Mackenzie's discomfort was making her uncomfortable, too.

"Shane," Donovan finally interceded, "I most humbly beg your forgiveness for the crass and unseemly behavior my ... wife ... has shown yours before this assembly of honored guests, and under the roof of your home. If it pleases you, may I ask that you leave her punishment up to me? I assure you, she will be dealt with harshly."

Mackenzie seemed to shake from the effort it took to keep her mouth shut.

Shane, enjoying his role, flicked his hand. "Take her. Do with her as you please."

Donovan retrieved his 'wife.' Mackenzie returned to her seat, dropping herself onto it with a scowl and a petulant grunt.

"Excellent, Donovan," Dr. Pendergast said. "Very well done. That was exactly how a true gentleman of Ancient Greece would have extracted his wife from a sticky social situation."

The bell rang, signaling the end of class and cutting Dr. Pendergast's praise short. "Have a wonderful Thanksgiving tomorrow," Dr. Pendergast said to the class. "I hope you all have room for turkey. I know I don't, after the way I ate this afternoon."

Mackenzie grabbed her books and bolted from the classroom. Candice was close behind her. The rest of the students left while Shane and Norm began disposing of the few leftovers—minus a few Must Rolls that Dr. Pendergast took with him. Charysse hung back to help.

"You called me 'Meli'," Charysse said as she stacked the abandoned plates. "I can't remember what that means."

Shane was a cultural contradiction as he cleared the table while wearing the tunic and armored chest and shin guards of a Greek warrior. "It's the Greek word for honey," he said. "I didn't use it properly, but it's close enough."

Charysse pressed back a smile. The word had been in one of the Greek cookbooks Shane had worked from. That's where she had seen it. Meli, she thought happily. As though they really were a married couple, he had called her 'Honey,' right there in front of everyone.

Charysse began to hum as she tossed empty juice cups into the trash bin.

CHAPTER SEVEN

Charysse stood sipping a glass of water at the sink in the McKenna kitchen. Norm's lamb nibbled at the potted chives Shane and his father had set in the frozen ground surrounding the doghouse in which the lamb now resided. The lamb occasionally poked its nose into the air and bleated, its breath forming ribbons of air in the cold. The forlorn sound echoed the way Charysse felt as she stood at the sink.

The McKenna house seemed too big, too cold and too empty without Shane. Charysse figured that he and his father were halfway to Foxboro, on their first father-son outing in more than five years.

Both father and son had almost begged out at the last minute, both dawdling once Charysse arrived. She had practically ushered them into their coats and into Mr. McKenna's Volvo before they'd been willing to stop worrying and entrust Mrs. McKenna to Charysse's care. But standing alone in the dim kitchen, Charysse had reservations of her own.

She emptied her glass, washed it, and propped it in the drying rack. She thought about calling Bonnie over, but decided against it. Bonnie was all noise and color and constant motion—she was the human equivalent of kryptonite to a depressed person.

"That's it," Charysse whispered, her skin prickling with anticipation as she thought of what she could do to occupy her time while the McKenna men were away. She trotted over to the tall bookcase and scanned the cookbooks. Finding the one most likely to have what she wanted, she searched the index for a cookie recipe. She smiled when she found it, and she started collecting the ingredients.

Charysse alternately sang softly and talked to herself as she measured, mixed, dolloped and baked. She had raised the lights over the prep island in the center of the room, and while her cookies baked, she sat at the island and watched the lamb scamper in the backyard. Shane hadn't told her that he was keeping it. But then, they hadn't spent much time alone over the past few days. Charysse had spent all of Thanksgiving Day with Bonnie's family and Marty, and Shane had dropped by for two hours after dinner. Charysse had spent Friday shopping with her mother since the two of them had spent little time together since Charysse's transfer to Eichorn. Shane stayed home all day Saturday. Charysse assumed that he was feeling guilty about going to the Pats game, and that he wanted to make it up to his mom in advance.

Charysse looked forward to the end of the game, when hopefully, she and Shane could have some alone time. She found herself staring at the pages of the cookbook and not seeing the words. Once she started thinking about Shane, it was impossible to turn her thoughts elsewhere. And she almost always thought of Shane.

The left side of her mouth rose in a shy grin when she pictured him in his Greek warrior's costume. He hadn't looked silly in his tunic, the way Bradley had. Shane's long, strong legs, still dark with a shadow of his summer tan, were his best feature. Until she'd seen the muscles of his arms flexing around the leather cords of his shield. Her heart had stopped for a good ten beats when he'd removed his cloak. Lotus's warrior's tunic was cut low on the sides, easily revealing the solid, sculpted muscle of Shane's sides and back.

Charysse would have mused on Shane's physique all the rest of the afternoon if the oven timer hadn't gone off, interrupting her pleasant daydream. She hurried to the oven, put on a pair of cow-shaped oven mitts, and pulled two cookie sheets from the oven. She set them on the cool stovetop. The scent of the cookies tantalized her nose but they were still too hot to eat.

She used a spatula to transfer the cookies from the baking sheets to cooling racks. Charysse, her back to the counter, was lightly bouncing one steaming cookie on her fingertips as she blew on it, to cool it, when she noticed a shadowy figure standing in the wide doorway connecting the kitchen to the corridor.

She continued to blow on the cookie even as the figure approached.

Mrs. McKenna didn't look the way she had in the photos on her book jackets. Her once black hair was streaked with silver that caught the golden light from the fixture above the prep island. Her blue eyes seemed larger and deeper, and her high cheekbones were too prominent. When she reached past Charysse for one of the cookies, her hands seemed too thin and frail to actually lift the weight of it.

"I was just about to bring your medication to you," Charysse said. She hoped that her voice didn't betray her surprise at seeing Mrs. McKenna out and about. Shane and his father had been sure that she would remain in her room. Charysse was fast believing that the McKenna men didn't know Mrs. McKenna the way they thought they did.

"I don't need it." Mrs. McKenna's voice was low and slightly raspy, is if from disuse. "You know that."

Charysse nibbled at the warm cookie. Mrs. McKenna took a tiny bite of her own. "What kind of cookies are these?" she asked.

"Chocolate chip," Charysse said.

Mrs. McKenna slowly ate her cookie. Her movements were slow and deliberate as she chewed and brushed crumbs from the front of her white robe.

"Would you like something to drink?" Charysse asked. She went to the refrigerator and pulled out a gallon of milk. "Or would you rather have tea or coffee or—"

"Milk is fine," Mrs. McKenna said. She glided over to the small white table in the breakfast nook and sat down. Charysse was aware of Mrs. McKenna's eyes on her as she poured two tall glasses of milk, set cookies on a plate, and brought them to the table. "You're Charysse," Mrs. McKenna said.

"Yes," she smiled. "Shane and Mr. McKenna went to a football game. They should be back around eight."

"And you were left here to babysit."

Charysse thought she saw a twinkle in Mrs. McKenna's dark brown eyes, but it may have been a trick of the light that barely spilled over into the breakfast nook. "I wanted to be here," Charysse said.

"My son speaks quite highly of you."

"He speaks highly of you, too," Charysse said.

"I think perhaps he tells me more than he otherwise would, since he believes that I'm too doped up to really know what he's saying," Mrs. McKenna said with a sad smile.

"He misses you," Charysse said.

Tears dotted Mrs. McKenna's lower lashes and she dropped her eyes to the cookie plate. "There are no chocolate chips in these cookies."

"I couldn't find any," Charysse smiled. "But the cookies are still good, aren't they?"

Mrs. McKenna wiped away a tear as she nodded and smiled. "They're the best chocolate chip cookies I've ever had."

"I read your book," Charysse said. She toyed with her thumbnail as she inwardly debated whether to pursue the subject she most wanted to discuss with Mrs. McKenna.

"Which book?" Mrs. McKenna asked. She gave her eyes a final wipe with the lapel of her robe.

"*Song For My Children*." Charysse's stomach tightened. "My mother bought it right after my father died. I read it, too. It..." She had to clear the lump that had sprung into her throat. "It helped us. It helped me get through it. Even now."

"I wish I could say the same thing." Mrs. McKenna turned her head and stared out of the window. Her face seemed as gray as the smoky clouds that now cloaked the sun.

"My memory isn't as good as Shane's, but something you wrote has stuck with me all these years," Charysse said. "'Life is such a miracle, both in getting here and staying here. I try to make myself believe that the life itself is what I should remember and treasure, not its duration. But I suppose it's my greedy nature that I want my angels close to me always, not up in Heaven.'"

"That book was written for my daughter. Marlys."

"But it's called *Song For My Children*," Charysse pointed out gently. "Plural. Both of your angels are close. One of them is within is reach. All you have to do is grab on to him. I know how hard that is because grief makes us selfish."

"Selfish?" Mrs. McKenna questioned.

"Sometimes we hurt so much we forget about everything but our own pain."

Mrs. McKenna rose and shuffled over to the paper towel rack mounted beside the sink. She tore off a few sheets and brought them to the table. "Shane was right about you."

"How so?"

"He told me that you had a way of seeing things for what they were. Shane also told me that your father was a therapist. The gift must be genetic."

"My mother tells me that I'm like him. I hope I am. He was..." She couldn't find the words to describe how loving, giving, kind, smart and funny her father was.

"Your father," Mrs. McKenna finished easily. "He was your angel."

"Would you like to see a picture of him?"

"Yes, of course," Mrs. McKenna said.

Charysse went into the foyer and took her jacket from the coat tree. She pulled her wallet from her pocket. When she returned to the kitchen, she squatted on Mrs. McKenna's side of the table and opened her wallet to the one photo of her father she always carried with her.

Mrs. McKenna brought the wallet closer to her face to get a better look at the photo. "You have his smile," she said. "And his eyes. I've never seen this shade of green before, except in Scotland. The moss that covers the bases of the black oaks is this vibrant shade of green. He's very handsome."

Charysse returned to her seat. "My mother said that the first time she saw him, her heart stopped because he was so good-looking. I just see him as my dad. I miss him so much sometimes, I just want to crawl into a hole and—"

"Lose yourself in misery," Mrs. McKenna said somberly. Then a corner of her mouth rose in a tiny grin. "Been there, done that."

"Do you have any pictures of your daughter?"

Mrs. McKenna's eyes widened, betraying her shock. Charysse was about to apologize, to beg forgiveness for her audacity, but Mrs. McKenna spoke before she could. "No one has ever asked to see Marlys," she said simply. "I'll get the pictures."

She stood and swept out of the kitchen, and Charysse would have sworn that Mrs. McKenna actually looked happy.

*

Charysse didn't know how long Shane and his father had been standing in the doorway before she looked up and noticed them. They wore twin expressions of surprise that made Mrs. McKenna giggle once she turned and saw them, too.

"Did you have a good time?" she asked.

"Yeah," Shane managed. He entered the now brightly lit kitchen, circling his mother as though she were an imposter. "We did. The Pats won, 38-16."

"Did you take your medication?" Mr. McKenna asked, his cheeks ruddy with November cold. He plucked off his polar fleece gloves and set them on the prep island.

Mrs. McKenna shared a glance with Charysse. "I'm off my meds, Geoff. I haven't taken them in months."

"Adrianna, what—" Mr. McKenna's words seemed to snag in his throat when he saw the photographs and albums spread out over the breakfast table. He slipped out of his coat and laid it across the back of an empty chair. He picked up one of the photos. Shane stood close to his father, studying the picture.

"Charysse was just helping me mount some photos," Mrs. McKenna said. "I think it's time I got these out of a shoebox and into an album properly."

Mr. McKenna only nodded. Still holding the photo, he set a hand on his wife's shoulder and gave it a meaningful squeeze. Mrs. McKenna placed her hand over her husband's, and rested her head upon it.

"Can I have one of these?" Shane asked as he intently studied one photo after another.

"I should be going now." Charysse felt totally out of place in the midst of the tender moment between Shane's parents. She started to leave when Mrs. McKenna stood up and hugged her, catching her completely by surprise.

"Thank you," Mrs. McKenna said, cupping Charysse's face in both hands. She hugged her again, holding her tightly and patting her back. "I'm glad Shane has a friend like you." Mrs. McKenna kissed each of her cheeks before turning her loose.

Charysse had just stepped out onto the front driveway when Shane trotted up to her. He was still wearing the dark blue fleece pullover he'd worn to the game, and the vivid color made his eyes appear their deepest, prettiest blue. "I don't know what you did, but thank you," he began. "I haven't seen her like this in years. She wants to make dinner. The last time she cooked dinner for us, my favorite meal was hotdogs and macaroni and cheese."

"I like her," Charysse said. "I just hope she doesn't slip back."

"If she does, I know what to do now," Shane said. "Call you."

An embarrassed smile came to Charysse's face. "You overestimate me."

"I don't think I do." Shane's breath condensed in the cold air.

"I told your mom about the Impressionists exhibit in Boston," Charysse said. "Maybe you should take her this week. Do it before she can change her mind about wanting to go."

"Will you go with us?"

"Maybe that's something you two should do together," Charysse gently suggested.

"Maybe," Shane said. He gave the end of Charysse's nose a light, playful touch. The impulsive gesture made Charysse giggle. He set his hands at her waist and drew her closer, touching his forehead to hers. "I don't know what I like better. The sound of your laugh or the way you look when you do it."

"Shane?"

He took a step back and turned to see his mother standing on the porch, pulling her robe closer about her in the cold. "Do you want your hotdogs grilled or boiled?"

"Either is fine, Mom," he called back. Color flamed in his cheeks. "Okay, so I still like hotdogs and macaroni and cheese."

"You should go back in and be with her," Charysse said. "With both of them."

"You can stay if you want. I'd like you to."

She looked away from him. "I have to get home. There's something I have to do."

"Sure," he said, his brow wrinkled in curiosity.

"She's great, you know," Charysse said as she unlocked her car door. "She loves you so much."

"I know." Shane opened the driver's door for her.

"I think that's why she withdrew," Charysse said. "She lost one child. It made her afraid to show how much she loved you, for fear of losing you, too. Have some of the chocolate chip cookies for dessert. You mom said they were the best she'd ever had. See you at school tomorrow." She got in the car and backed out of the driveway. When she looked back in her rear view mirror, Shane was still in the driveway, staring after her.

*

The loud knocking on the front door startled Charysse, but when she looked through the peephole on her front door and saw Shane, a different kind of fear washed through her. She unlocked the door and invited him in, but he remained on the porch. Only then did Charysse notice the serious set of his handsome features. His face looked like a cloudy sky before a big storm. Charysse was dressed in old cut-offs and an oversized sweatshirt, but the cold breeze on her bare legs wasn't what gave her goosebumps as she held Shane's intense gaze.

"Hi," she said warily. "Is something wrong? Is your mom okay?"

Sadness crept into his face. He seemed to be having trouble working out an answer. He shoved his hands into the pockets of his jeans and stared past her. She reached for him, and he shirked away. "Shane?" she said, her alarm climbing a notch.

He pinned his eyes on her. They flashed with a brilliant blue burst of anger. "Who do you think you are?"

There was no rancor or bitterness in his tone, but the sadness in his voice wounded her. "I don't understand," she said.

He shoved a photo at her. "You went too far this time!"

Charysse looked at the picture of a dark-haired young man in jeans and athletic shoes sitting in a rocking chair. The bed and curtain in the background marked the setting as a hospital room. Charysse couldn't make out the face of the blanket-swathed bundle in pink on the young man's lap, but she was sure that it was Marlys.

"You had no right to put that in my room!" Shane charged.

"Shane, I—"

"Why couldn't you leave well enough alone?" he went on, his misery apparent in every word he spoke and every stilted movement. "You can't make people live the way you want them to. I told you I never met my sister, so you had to dig this photo up and ambush me with it." He abruptly turned away from her. Charysse thought he was leaving, so she went after him. He stopped at the top step of the porch. The moonlight shimmered in the moisture rimming his lower lashes. Charysse touched his back. When he spoke again, his voice was thick with unshed tears. "I forgot about that picture. I forgot about that day." He shook his head. "How could I have forgotten?" he whispered anxiously. "I *remember*. That's what I do. But I forgot that I'd ever held her, that I'd listened to her heartbeat and that I'd heard her cry and snore and burp." He pinched his eyes with his thumb and forefinger, but the gesture didn't stop his tears from coming. "As long as I didn't remember her, I didn't have to mourn her."

Charysse hugged him from behind, standing on her tiptoes to bring her chin even with his shoulder. "I'm so sorry, Shane. I told your mom that you'd mentioned that you'd never met your sister, but I didn't put that photo in your room. I've never been in your room."

Shane spun in her embrace and slid his arms around her. He buried his face in her hair. "I'm sorry I yelled at you and blamed you."

"It's okay. I'm a busybody and I know it." Charysse shivered. She didn't know if it was because of the chilly air on her skin or because of the way Shane's heartbeat felt against hers.

"You should go back inside," he said. "You're freezing."

He led her into her house and offered to make coffee or hot cocoa to warm her up. They made hot cocoa together and took it into the study. "What's going on in here?" Shane asked when he saw half-filled, open boxes everywhere.

"I'm packing away my father's things," she answered simply. She glanced around the room rather than at Shane. "You didn't remember. I remember too much. Your mom kind of showed me that I can let go of these things without letting go of my dad."

"You've been crying," he observed, peering at her face.

"There's been a lot of that going around tonight," she chuckled lightly.

"Want some help packing?" he asked.

She shook her head. "Mom will probably help me. I think it would be good for us to pack this room up together. If there's something you want, please, take it."

Shane leaned on the desk. He ran a finger over the polished lid of the humidor. Charysse swooped in and scooped it up. She hugged the box to her chest. "Except this." Tears blurred Shane's image, but she didn't let the tears fall. "I'm keeping this."

He cupped her face in one hand. "Is that enough?"

She nodded. "It will be, from now on."

*

Norm, with his peculiar, crab-like gait, skittered down the corridor. He walked with his back to the rows of lockers to avoid making any sort of physical contact with anyone, and judging by his speed, he was late for his second period Quantum Physics Lab. Charysse, who had a free period, was standing at her locker with Lotus when Norm zoomed by.

"Norm is one weird cat," Charysse said as she worked the combinations on the two combination locks she'd used on her locker ever since the Lemke paper incident. When Lotus gasped and shouted "Oh my God!", Charysse realized that two combination locks offered little challenge to an Eichorn student.

Someone had again invaded her locker, only this time it was to put something in rather than take something out. Situated on the shelf of her locker was an elegant vase filled with a wild arrangement of roses, baby sunflowers, spray mums, Bells of Ireland, baby's breath, and a host of other blossoms Charysse couldn't name. Small clusters of Prof. Roentgen's hybrid grapes accentuated the bouquet, and Charysse knew exactly who had given her the flowers. A small white envelope dangled from a pretty bow of white satin and tulle tied around the neck of the vase.

"Open the card!" Lotus urged. Her bright smile was the perfect complement to the skin-tight, violet, white and black Pucci dress she wore. To Charysse, she looked like an extra from an Austin Powers movie.

Lotus held the bouquet and examined it from all sides while Charysse opened the card. "I'd love to do a watercolor of this arrangement," Lotus said. "My Painting final is due in three weeks, and this would be perfect."

"Be my guest," Charysse said absently. She was distracted by the contents of the envelope, a little note that read:

I know this isn't much compared to what you've given me. Consider it a thank you, and an apology for the way I acted last night.

Beneath the turkey-scratch handwriting was Shane's name. Charysse closed the tiny card into her hand for a moment before she tucked it into an inner pocket of her book satchel. By the time she withdrew from her own orbit of contentment to focus her attention on Lotus's ongoing commentary, a bunch of junior and senior girls had gathered around her.

"Are these from Shane?" Lotus asked. " 'Cause if they're not, you're gonna have some serious explaining to do when he hears about them."

"They're from Shane," Charysse confirmed.

A chorus of gooey "Awws," rose from Charysse's onlookers.

"They're really pretty," came a soft voice from the edge of the crowd.

"Candice," Charysse said, reaching through the crowd to pull Candice forward. One of the girls yelped when one of Candice's big, chunky shoes landed on her instep.

Charysse's eyes widened for an instant when she took in Candice's entire ensemble. Along with the clunky shoes that gave her an extra two inches of height, her skinny legs were wrapped in clingy stretch denim jeans that flared at the cuffs. She wore a low-cut, knit top that emphasized the prominence of her collarbones. As was her new habit, she was wearing a full mask of heavy makeup. Her hair was pulled into a simple ponytail, which drew attention to the contacts she now wore to turn her brown eyes violet.

Lotus couldn't help but shake her head when she met Charysse's gaze.

"You're so lucky, Charysse," Candice said. "No one has ever given me flowers."

"Candy!"

"See ya 'round, Candice," Lotus drawled as Candice again fought her way through the crowd, this time to answer Mackenzie's call. Candice fell in line behind Mackenzie and her friends and the foursome walked off.

"If you want to paint those, you can take them with you to the art building," Charysse said to Lotus, who perched the vase on her hip.

"Don't you want to take them home?" Lotus asked.

Charysse closed her locker and snapped the combination locks. "I don't need all of them. Besides, if you paint them, they'll last forever."

"Cool," Lotus said. "You can have the painting after it's graded. Deal?"

"Deal," Charysse agreed. She plucked three roses, a carnation, a fern, a cluster of baby's breath and a bunch of grapes with their leaves and vines intact from the vase.

"That's all you want?" Lotus said.

"This is all I need." Charysse started for the girls' bathroom, to get a damp paper towel to wrap around the cut ends of the flowers.

*

Charysse was sitting in Lindy's class, talking quietly with Shane, Lotus, Marty and Chrysanthemum when a clump of wet, wilted flowers landed on her desktop.

"You're something else," Mackenzie said, propping her little pink fist on her hip as she waved a perfectly manicured finger at Charysse. "Shane gives you flowers and you flaunt them in poor Candy's face."

Charysse released a weary sigh and braced herself for yet another encounter with Mackenzie and her ego. "That wasn't flaunting, it was sharing." Charysse leaned to one side, to see Candice past Mackenzie. "I didn't mean any insult to you, Candice. You know that, don't you?"

"I know," Candice said in a small voice.

"Shut up, Candy!" Mackenzie sneered.

"I gave those flowers to Candice because she said she liked them," Charysse said. "Why can't you just let her enjoy them?"

"How is she supposed to enjoy some other girl's leftovers?" Mackenzie said. "You think she's so pathetic that that's the only way she'll ever get flowers?"

"Actually," Charysse said coolly, "that's probably what you think."

"Sit down, Mac," Marty said. "You're giving me a headache. As usual."

"I think you're all bent because Charysse and Candice got flowers from Shane and you didn't," Lotus said.

Mackenzie shifted her feral stare to Lotus. "You wish! And Candice didn't get anything from Shane."

"If I'd known that she liked flowers so much, I would have given her some," Shane said casually.

Candice blushed fiercely. She shrank deep in her seat and hid her face behind a three-ring binder.

"Class," Ms. Lindy interrupted, reminding them that she was still in the room, "if you could put your little squabble on hold for a moment, I'd like to discuss something only slightly more significant. A Christmas party."

"Party!" Bradley piped.

"I know that the senior class is already planning some sort of on-campus affair for the day before Christmas Break, but I was hoping we could have a party just for our class," Ms. Lindy said.

"Could we call it a Holiday Party instead of a Christmas party?" Bradley asked. "I'm Jewish. I don't do Christmas."

"Call it whatever you like," Ms. Lindy said. "You have three weeks to think about it. I suggest a sign-up sheet for food, beverages, paper goods, and—"

"I still have Lemke's Treasure," Charysse said. "I could use it to pay for the party. Maybe we could all go out for dinner or something on the last day of the term. We could rent a couple of limos and really make a big deal of it."

"Can we bring dates?" Marty asked.

"That's a good question," Charysse said, a mischievous twinkle in her eyes, "who do you have in mind, Marty?" Charysse knew perfectly well that Marty and Bonnie were official, but she couldn't resist having a little fun at Marty's expense.

"I vote for the Empire Garden in Chinatown," Donovan said. "They have the best dim sum in town, plus I can practice my Mandarin."

"No Chinese," Charysse said. "Too risky for Chrysanthemum. She's allergic to nuts and there's cashews and peanuts and peanut oil at Chinese restaurants."

"Italian's good for me, too," Donovan said.

"Then that's settled," Ms. Lindy smiled. "I'm actually looking forward to it."

"Ms. Lindy?" Mackenzie said sweetly as she raised her right hand. "I think I have a better idea."

Ms. Lindy crooked a fine eyebrow, waiting for Mackenzie's offer. Mackenzie, prolonging her time in the spotlight, spent a moment wriggling her hips in her tight leather skirt. "My parents have given me permission to have a party at our beach house on the Cape. It'll be catered, of course, and they'll probably charter a bus to take everyone there and back. It'll be an overnight and a lot of fun. You're welcome to help my parents chaperone, Ms. Lindy."

"We were talking about doing something with just the Lindy class and you know it," Shane said. "Who else are you planning to invite?"

"I have a very select guest list in mind," Mackenzie smirked.

"Who's for a Lindy class party?" Lotus asked. "Hands?"

All hands went up, except for Mackenzie's. Candice's went down when Mackenzie glared at her.

"I can still have a party at my beach house," Mackenzie said. "Candice, take names. Donovan, I can count you in, can't I?"

"I'm booked through New Year's," Donovan said. "Sorry."

"Lotus," Mackenzie said. "And Chrysanthemum...I know we haven't been the best of friends, but—"

"You called us 'genetic hiccups,'" Chrysanthemum reminded her without looking up from the book she was reading.

"I don't like sand," Lotus smiled.

"I can come," Bradley said. "Name the day."

Mackenzie's face pulled into a mask of disgust. "Fine. There are plenty of people who'd love to come to the Cape over break."

"Summer break, maybe," Donovan said. "Christmas break, I don't know..."

"The Cape is beautiful any time of year," Charysse said. "It's nice to sit inside with a fire crackling on the hearth, staring out at the waves breaking on shore. It's cozy."

Shane rested his hand on the back of Charysse's chair.

"Who asked for your opinion?!" Mackenzie nearly shrieked. "You're not invited anyway!"

"Miss Cole!" Ms. Lindy snapped. "Control yourself!"

"I never assumed that I was invited," Charysse said calmly. "In fact, I think you brought up this whole beach house thing just to make yourself the center of attention. To try to make people envy you the way you envy me."

Mackenzie laughed and it was a dry, brittle, forced sound. "Is that so? I envy you?"

"There's no other explanation for the way you behave around me," Charysse said. "At first I thought you were just hateful by nature, and you are to a large extent. But you save your very worst for me. I think you're the kind of person who hates what she covets."

"You're just some poor dump of a girl from Lesterville," Mackenzie laughed. "What could you possibly have that I want?"

Charysse held Mackenzie's mean stare. "Do you really want me to say right here, in front of the whole class?"

"If you're talking about Shane," she said icily, "every boy goes through a slumming phase."

"This isn't about Shane and you know it," Charysse said. "This is about you, me, and why you can't seem to stop messing with my life and start trying to fix your own."

Mackenzie stared at Charysse as though she could make her disappear through wishful thinking alone. Mackenzie looked away first. "Keep your stupid observations to yourself because I couldn't care less what you think." With that, Mackenzie flounced back to her desk and sat down.

"So," Marty said, drawing the word out cheerfully, "are we doin' Italian, or what?"

Chapter Eight

"I turned my painting in yesterday," Lotus said as she tipped her head back to rinse her hair in the steaming water of the shower. "It's called, 'Still Life with Fruit and Flora.' I have my grading session with Dr. Lithgow and the grading panel at four."

In the adjoining stall, Charysse turned off her shower and squeezed water from her long hair. "Grading sessions scare me to death. The only one I had this semester was for my American Literature class. I had to sit there in front of three professors and defend the paper I wrote on *Billy Budd*. I totally sounded like an idiot." Charysse pulled her towel from its resting place across the top of the stall door. She wrapped it tightly around her before stepping out of the shower stall.

Lotus, wearing nothing but a pair of neon pink flip-flops, was waiting for her outside the stall. She used a corner of her fluffy white towel to dry her right ear before she wrapped the towel around her head turban style and walked with Charysse to their lockers.

"I wish I had your confidence," Charysse said. The other girls, accustomed to Lotus's comfort with her own nudity, didn't spare a glance at Lotus's pale body as she moved through the locker room.

"It's just skin," Lotus said with a shrug. "And hair and moles."

"You make it sound ugly when you have to know how gorgeous you are." Charysse stopped at the bench in front of her gym locker. "It's funny how Chrysanthemum practically showers in her clothes while you're perfectly comfortable letting it all hang out."

"Speaking of hanging out," Lotus said as she opened her locker, "is everything set for the Lindy party?"

Charysse perked up. "I've never planned a big party before because I could never afford to have one. I didn't know how much fun it would be. Two stretch limos are going to pick everyone up at their houses on Wednesday night and take us to the North End. We're either going to Polcari's, or Davio's in Boston. I made reservations at each, and I figured we could vote in class tomorrow on which place we want to go to. I'll just cancel the one we don't need."

"You're too much, Charysse," Lotus said as she drew on a tiny pair of pink panties. "I would have long spent Lemke's Treasure. Will you have enough money to cover it?"

Charysse nodded. "I threw in some of my trivia winnings, just in case. I invited Dr. Lemke, too. He actually said that he would come."

Lotus snorted. "He'd go anywhere Ms. Lindy went. Half the faculty has the hots for her."

Charysse sat beside Lotus on the bench while Lotus slipped on a very conservative white button-down shirt. But then Charysse saw that the entire back of the shirt was missing, from the base of the collar to Lotus's waist. "You know who else I think likes Ms. Lindy?" Charysse said.

"Who?"

"Norm."

Lotus laughed out loud. "Norm is an alien."

"I thought he was born in Malden," Charysse joked.

"That's where the mothership *landed*," Lotus said dryly. "Norm doesn't have regular, human emotions. I've never seen him even talk to a girl, let alone make goo-goo eyes at one."

"Have you ever noticed how he gets still whenever Ms. Lindy looks at him or talks to him lately?" Charysse said. "The first time I noticed it, I thought I was just imagining it."

"Norm's a perpetual motion machine," Lotus said.

"Watch him next time we're in class," Charysse advised.

"Watching him makes me tired." Lotus buttoned her sweeping, floor-length black skirt and tugged on a pair of Mary Poppins-style lace-up ankle boots. "I have to go. The art department heads are pretty loose when it comes to everything but grading sessions."

Charysse stood and watched Lotus elegantly move through the crowded locker room. "Good luck with 'Still Life with Fruit and Flora!'" she called after her. Certain that the beautiful painting would earn Lotus her highest artistic accolades ever, Charysse opened her locker. The happiness she felt for her friend drained away when she saw that her clothes were no longer in her locker.

Loud giggling from the next aisle of lockers sent a bolt of anger lancing through Charysse as she slammed her locker shut. "Is there some Evil Stereotype Handbook you work from?" Charysse demanded as she stormed into the next aisle and singled Mackenzie out from amidst her likely co-conspirators. "My clothes had better be back in my locker by the time I get back from Coach Zanca's office."

Mackenzie, who was using the mirror affixed to her locker door, stopped applying a fresh coat of mascara. "You're actually going to tell the athletic director on me?" she giggled. "What a baby."

Bea and Leslie, each dressed in blue jeans and tight sweaters that matched Mackenzie's, whispered under their breath and laughed at Charysse.

Charysse closed her eyes in a long blink of frustration and impatience. "I should have known that the peace you've given me over the past three weeks was just too good to be true. I should have known that you'd pull something this close to the end of the term. Well, guess what, Big Mac? You can still get busted for stealing my personal property." Charysse turned and started for the door that led directly to Coach Zanca's office.

Mackenzie followed close on her heels. "Can you prove that I took your clothes? Maybe I should tell on you, for falsely accusing *me*. Maybe I'll just come along to the office with you."

Mackenzie's entourage, which included a silent and somber Candice, trailed them. "I'm sick of you, Mackenzie," Charysse said as they approached the locked double doors that joined the girls locker room to the weight room. "I'm sick of your stupid, immature sh—"

Charysse's last word was masked by the sudden screech and whoosh of the double doors opening on their rarely used hinges. Before she could register what was happening, Charysse found herself surrounded by laughing faces and felt hands clawing at her body. In the next instant, she was stumbling backwards, her damp skin goosepimpling in the cool air generated by the movement of her towel as it was yanked from her body. She landed hard on her tailbone on the springy, rubberized floor of the weight room. The last thing she saw, as the double doors were pulled shut, was Mackenzie's laughing face.

*

The next few seconds seemed to last for years.

Nausea swirled in Charysse's head and gut as she plastered herself to the doors and tried to pull them open. The cold metal bars of the door handles seemed to burn into her damp flesh. She could hear laughter from the other side of the door, and the sound of the floor bolts being activated.

"No way!" came an unknown male voice from behind her. The heat of embarrassment set her skin on fire as she peeped over her shoulder. Icy droplets of water from her wet hair ran down her arms and back as she saw junior and senior boys and their coaches on the various weight machines. One by one they seemed to take notice of her. Machines and sweating bodies came to a stop. Some of the boys stared at her in wide-eyed, open-mouthed shock. Other boys smiled, caught laughter in their hands, or lightly applauded.

Charysse couldn't breathe. Her muscles tightened as she tried to cover herself with her hands and arms. She was in the open, trapped at the back of the weight room. The only way out was straight ahead, past dozens of machines, past the free weight arena, and past the treadmills and exercise bikes. When a deep, male chuckle reached her ears, Charysse froze in sick humiliation. She sank to the floor, shielding herself as best as she could, hoping she could die right there on the spot.

"Come on," she heard distantly as she felt movement over her. Too numb to cry or speak, Charysse simply obeyed as Shane crouched over her, blocking her from the eyes fixed on them. He took off his sweatshirt and helped her into it. The sleeves of the garment swallowed her arms and covered her to the middle of her thighs. As if she were a child, he scooped her up and set her on her feet. She hid her face in his T-shirt. Shane clapped an arm around her shoulders and steered her down the aisle. The silence of the boys and the equipment was almost as unpleasant as their whispers and laughter had been as Shane ushered her out of the weight room and into the foyer of the gymnasium.

Once she was out of public view, Charysse wrapped her arms around Shane's neck. Shouts, cheers, applause and laughter erupted in the weight room. It stopped only when one of the coaches blew his whistle and ordered the boys back to their workouts.

Charysse drew in deep, heaving breaths that did nothing to relieve the churning in her belly or clear away her lightheadedness. "Shane," she murmured. Beyond tears, beyond anger, she couldn't say anything other than his name. His arms tightened around her, shielding her, protecting her, comforting her. "I have to go home," she whimpered. "I want to go home right now."

"What happened?" Shane asked. "Mackenzie?"

"I just want to go home." Her voice was stubborn and flat, even to her own ears. She was sure that she sounded perfectly crazy to him.

"Let's get your clothes," he said. Holding her hand firmly, he led her to the entrance of the girls' locker room. He didn't hesitate before he walked right in, pulling Charysse behind him. There were a few girls in the locker room, and even though they were dressed, they squawked at the sight of Shane. "What's your locker number?" he asked Charysse.

"424," she said.

Shane found it and opened it. Charysse's clothes had returned. Only now they were soaking wet. Shane took off his sweatpants, leaving himself dressed only in his Eichorn gym shorts, T-shirt, socks and cross trainers. He gave the pants to Charysse, who put them on in a wordless daze. "Mr. Kennedy is probably still on campus," Shane said. "You have to go to him and tell him what Mackenzie did this time. Tell him how she's been harassing you since school started."

"I just want to go home!" Charysse yelled tearfully. Her tone softened. "Can't I just go home and forget about this?"

"I'll drive you." Shane reached under the sweatshirt and hiked up the sweatpants, which were too long and too wide for her slender frame. "I'll run home and get the car. It'll take me five minutes, I promise."

"I can call Bonnie."

"Would you just think about talking to Mr. Kennedy?"

"No! I don't want anyone else to know…" She bit her lip to force back tears. "They saw me. They all saw me."

Shane clapped his arms around her and hugged her to his chest. He pressed his lips to her hair and stroked her back.

"Excuse me, Miss DiGregorio, Mr. McKenna, but you have ten seconds to explain what's going on here."

Charysse pulled away from Shane, but he remained close to her as if he had to protect her from Coach Zanca, who stood before them with her large hands curled on her hips. "It's not what you think, Coach," Charysse said.

Coach Zanca narrowed her pale blue eyes at Charysse's face before scanning Shane. "How do you know what I'm thinking?"

Shane reached into Charysse's locker and took out her clothes. He plopped the sodden mess at the coach's feet. "Someone stole Charysse's clothes while she was in the shower and then pushed her into the weight room. This is how we found her clothes just now."

Coach Zanca's angular face softened. "Is that what all the hooting and cheering was about a few minutes ago?"

Charysse sat heavily on the bench, hugging her middle. Coach Zanca dropped to one knee beside her and laid a gentle hand on her forearm. "Who did this, Charysse?"

"I don't know."

"It was Mackenzie Cole," Shane spat. "She's been on Charysse's case since September."

"I don't know who took my clothes," Charysse said, her tone flat and empty. "I can't prove that it was Mackenzie. I'm going home now." She bent over and picked up her wet bundle of clothes.

"This isn't something I'm going to brush off as a harmless prank," Coach Zanca said. "Whoever did this to you, Charysse, is going to be held accountable."

"I can't prove that Mackenzie took my clothes, but she was definitely the one who took my towel and shoved me into the weight room. Beatrice Smolley, Leslie Pass, and Candice James helped her. I was on my way to your office when it happened because I wanted my clothes back. I have them, and now, I'm going home."

Coach Zanca took the wet clothing. "Let me keep these, Charysse. Just for a little while."

"Fine." Charysse stood. The too-large pants almost stayed behind. "I don't care. I have to call someone to pick me up." She started away and Shane started after her. "Don't," she pleaded, stopping him. "Just let me go, please?"

Charysse kept walking, out of the locker room, out of the gymnasium, and right off campus. Only when she was a half of a mile away, at a pay phone outside a pharmacy, did she stop and call Bonnie to come and get her out of Wakefield and away from Eichorn.

*

Charysse didn't answer the phone, which rang continually until past ten. She lay in her bed, curled up in Shane's sweats, feeling as though her nerve endings didn't quite touch the surface of her skin. Inside, though, her chest burned with a mixture of anger, hurt and humiliation. She had fallen asleep, but didn't realize she had done so until she woke up to her mother's soft voice.

"What time is it?" Charysse asked, groggy with sleep.

"A little after one," Karen DiGregorio told her daughter. "Your headmaster called me at work tonight but I didn't get the message until midnight. I woke him up when I returned his call, but since he left his home number, I thought it was important."

Charysse gazed up at her mother's face. Her mother had married at twenty and given birth to Charysse a year later. Karen DiGregorio looked younger than her thirty-nine years and was often mistaken for Charysse's sister, rather than her mother. But tonight, in the dim wash of moonlight in the room, Charysse saw that her mother's chestnut hair had scant strands of gray that caught the silver light, and she made out a new crop of fine wrinkles in her mother's brow.

"What happened at school today?" Mrs. DiGregorio asked.

The tender inquiry pulled at Charysse's heart. She saw her own pain mirrored in her mother's eyes. She rolled onto her side, refusing to cry in front of her mother. Mrs. DiGregorio, still dressed in the dark green blazer that comprised her Save 'N Shop manager's uniform, climbed into bed with Charysse. She hugged her daughter, pressing Charysse's back to her chest. Charysse's closed her eyes and lost herself to her mother's touch as she stroked her hair.

"You totally deprived me of your childhood, do you know that?" Mrs. DiGregorio said. "You never acted like a baby, even when you were a baby. You were fourteen months old when I caught you changing your own diaper. When you were six, you used to pull a chair up to the kitchen counter so make your own lunch, and you always made sure that each food group was represented. Especially the chocolate and sugar groups."

A quiet chuckle managed to find its way past the misery choking Charysse's spirit.

"When your father died," Mrs. DiGregorio said, "you picked up the pieces when I couldn't. You made sure the bills were paid, that there was food in the house, you did your homework and got yourself to school on time. You were a sixth-grader and you took care of me when I should have been taking care of you."

"Mom, don't."

"I'm sorry, love." Mrs. DiGregorio held Charysse tighter. "Since I went back to work, I assumed that you would come to me if you ever needed me."

"I always needed you, Mom. But I understood why you had to take the night job. It paid a lot more than the day shift."

"Why didn't you call me after gym today?"

"I called Bonnie. She picked me up and stayed here with me. She left while I was asleep, I guess."

"Charysse, honey...why didn't you call _me_?"

A backlog of unshed tears clogged her voice as she answered. "I didn't want you to know how stupid I am." When her mother started to interrupt, Charysse spoke over her. "I should have seen it coming. I walked right into it. Mackenzie showed me what she was capable of a long time ago, when she stole Lemke's paper."

"She did what?"

"It doesn't matter now, Mom. She's been riding me since I started at Eichorn."

"Maybe I should give her mother a call," Mrs. DiGregorio said. "Mr. Kennedy said that the school will handle it, but if this has been going on all semester, it's time the parents got involved."

"Please don't, Mom. Bonnie already wants to shave Mackenzie's eyebrows off for me. I can take care of this myself. Tomorrow. In Ms. Lindy's class."

"Let me be the mom this time, Charysse."

"You've always been my mom. You're a great mother. That's why I know I can fix this myself. Because I know I have you in my corner." For the first time since she left school, Charysse felt her strength returning. In her mother's arms, she no longer felt weakened by embarrassment. She was still angry, but even that she was able to channel into something constructive rather than self-pitying. "I can handle this, Mom. And I will."

*

Charysse moved through the next day in a state of semi-shock. She was aware of the way students suddenly quieted when she entered a classroom, and the way their eyes tracked her as she moved. Lunch had been nearly unbearable with Marty and the Achearn twins being aggressively attentive and kind while the rest of the cafeteria buzzed with conversation, most of it seemingly about her since the volume was lower than usual.

She had anxiously worked through her French and Music Appreciation finals, both dreading and looking forward to Lindy's class. Dreading it because of Mackenzie, longing for it because with Shane's revised testing, Lindy's class would be the only time she would see him.

By her own design, Charysse was the last student to walk into Lindy's class. The room went silent and still as she walked through it, to the seat Shane had saved for her. She felt the weight of the class's stares as she opened her satchel and pulled out Shane's neatly washed and folded sweatpants.

"I'm keeping the sweatshirt." Her even, pleasant voice broke the silence.

Shane gave her a quiet, adoring smile. "I don't mind. You look great in it."

"You look great out of it, too," Donovan said.

Marty shot out of his seat. "You're an ass, Donovan!" he shouted as Shane launched in with, "Grow up!"

"It's a compliment," Donovan argued innocently while Shane and Marty ranted at him. Charysse cringed against a renewed sense of humiliation. Norm's constant motion grew more pronounced in the chaos of voices and the twins tried to calm the boys. Candice began to weep while Mackenzie laughed.

No one noticed Ms. Lindy in the room until she loudly slammed her briefcase down on her desktop. She opened it and withdrew a clear plastic bag full of clothing. She marched over to Mackenzie's desk at the back of the classroom and emptied the soggy pile onto the desktop. Her upper lip curled in disgust, Mackenzie pushed her chair back.

The room instantly quieted. Marty and Donovan sat back down. Lotus and Chrysanthemum stopped speaking mid-word. Charysse was alarmed at the fiery gleam in Ms. Lindy's eyes and the rigid set of her delicate features.

"You little...!" she began in a snarl, before finishing with a word Charysse had certainly heard before, but not from the lips of a teacher in a classroom. Not even at Lesterville, where a substitute teacher had broken down under the pressure and ran from the building firing F-bombs and S-bombs.

"Ms. Lindy dropped an A-bomb," Donovan snickered, oblivious to the charged climate in the room.

"Quiet, Donovan!" Ms. Lindy fired, making him flinch. Her arms crossed angrily over her the front of her black shirt, she stood at the front of her desk. Her furious gaze fell on each of her students. "I just came from a meeting with Mr. Kennedy. I'm sure you geniuses can guess what that meeting was about."

Charysse looked up from her lap, expecting Ms. Lindy's eyes to be on her. They weren't.

"I know for a fact that everyone in this room was involved, in some way, and now you're all going to pay for the judgment calls you made."

Bradley stuck a wavering hand in the air. "Ms. Lindy," he argued nervously, "I didn't do anything. I was sitting there on the vertical arm press and all of a sudden ... there she was." Bradley's face turned vermillion as he stole a peek at Charysse.

"Do you hear yourself, Bradley?" Ms. Lindy asked. "'I didn't do anything.' That was a judgment call. Think before you speak the next time you want to give testimony regarding your culpability."

Ms. Lindy began to pace the row between the two sets of desks. Norm's rapidly tapping feet provided a strange musical accompaniment to the teacher's movements. "I think it's time that I told you what I teach here, what this class is all about. I don't teach so much as I observe and allow you to teach yourselves. You see, with great power comes great responsibility. Your intelligence makes you all very powerful. That's why I chose each of you for this class.

"There are thirteen categories of genius measured by I.Q. tests. To one degree or another, you all qualify as geniuses. On paper. This class is a test of your character. We won't prepare you intellectually for what awaits you beyond Eichorn without making sure that you have the maturity and decency to use your intelligence appropriately. To the best of our ability, we want to ensure that you each have caring and empathetic hearts to temper the capabilities of your super-powered brains."

"It was just supposed to be a prank." Candice's voice barely reached past the end of her desk. "It was a joke. Mackenzie didn't mean for it to get so blown out of proportion."

"Would you just shut up!?" Mackenzie hissed.

Ms. Lindy, wielding her index finger like a weapon, stomped in Mackenzie's direction. "You shut up, Miss Cole," she said darkly. "If I hear one more word from you, so help me, this will be your last day at Eichorn."

Mackenzie's lips pinched into a tight little ball of fury.

Ms. Lindy continued to address the class. "I teach students how to think for themselves. I teach them accountability." She spared a withering glance at Mackenzie. "Unfortunately, my lessons are only as good as my students." Ms. Lindy went to her desk and closed her briefcase. "You'll be grading yourselves in my class. I expect to see each of you here first period tomorrow, and you'd better have your grade and your defense of it prepared."

Mackenzie pushed the wet clothes onto the floor. "When I tell my parents what you said in class today, it'll be *your* last day at Eichorn."

Ms. Lindy slowly turned around to face Mackenzie. Charysse thought the teacher had grown a few inches taller in the time it took her to walk from her desk to the middle of the classroom. "Is there a chance that when I tell your parents what you did yesterday, they'll be as pissed off at you as I am?"

Mackenzie vaulted to her feet. "No matter what I did or didn't do, you have no right to talk to us like this. I can't wait for you to get fired. I'll laugh my head off, knowing that you're downtown in line for an unemployment check."

Ms. Lindy shook her head in amazement. "You're all Intuition and no perspective, Miss Cole, which is why you can't see what's really going on here. I'm independent of Eichorn. If I walk away from this job, I have a writing career to fall back on. If I don't want to write, I can consult for human resource firms, justice departments and psychology centers all over this country. My life is not this job and my life is in place. Do you seriously believe that a swear word will ruin me? I used words. You, on the other hand, acted. You did something cruel and vicious and wrong. The legacy of that action will follow you for the rest of your life because it revealed who – and what – you are. I can't help you any more. I sincerely hope that you at least try to help yourself."

"Do you know who my father is?" Mackenzie countered, her voice high and thin. "He's on Eichorn's board of directors.

This isn't over. Not by a long shot. He's got the power to ruin you, just like you're trying to ruin me."

"Your father had the power to convince me to accept you into this class because he thought you would benefit from it. Does he have the power to restore what you threw away yesterday?"

"You make no sense whatsoever," Mackenzie laughed bitterly. "You're like some high-functioning retard who speaks in her own language. What – in English, please – did I throw away?"

"Dignity. Maturity. Compassion. Class. That was English, but I suspect you don't understand any of those words."

Charysse watched Mackenzie silently fume as Ms. Lindy returned to her desk. She kept her back to the class as she spoke to them once more. This time, she sounded more tired than angry. "You people are supposed to be special. You're supposed to be gifted. But that doesn't make you any better than anyone else. You're all a talented group of kids but I see only one true genius among you. This is a student who excels because of hard work, not because of some genetic twist. This is a student who has shown dignity and strength that most of you will never have or understand, because you're too stubborn, too immature or just too dumb. Eichorn has an obligation to turn you loose on the world with your emotional and social maturation on a par with your intellect, and that's no different from any other school in this country. Most of you glow. One of you shines. And one of you is tarnished beyond repair."

Ms. Lindy snapped her briefcase shut. "I want your grades tomorrow. Class dismissed." She turned, her briefcase in hand. "Except for you, Miss Cole. Mr. Kennedy wishes to see you in his office. Since you're so fond of ambushes, I believe your father is already there."

CHAPTER NINE

Since there were no Homerooms during the three-day finals week, Ms. Lindy's classroom should have been empty during Tuesday's first period. Instead, her eighth period *Lindy: 401* students sat in the same desks they had occupied the previous afternoon. At 8:30 am sharp, they looked up as one when Ms. Lindy entered the room in a black and heather-grey wool suit that made her look more like a secret agent than a high school teacher. To the class's surprise, Mr. Kennedy was with her. He greeted the class before taking a seat beside Ms. Lindy at her desk.

"Let's get this over with," Ms. Lindy said. She shuffled a sheaf of papers in her hands and took up her marking pen. "Who would like to go first?"

Charysse looked around the classroom and saw that her friends were doing the same. No one looked as if they'd gotten a good night's sleep, and Bradley actually had to stifle a yawn in his fist. Grades were the ultimate challenge, reward and currency at Eichorn. Placing the status of their all-important GPA's into their own hands was an almost Biblical sort of punishment. Charysse knew how hard she had wrestled with her own grade, and now saw that everyone else had, too.

Except for Mackenzie. She was as alert and bright-eyed as a fox trailing a wounded chicken.

Just when it seemed as if Ms. Lindy would have to start calling on people, Norm stood up. Shifting his weight from foot to foot as he tapped his left fist against his hip, he cleared his throat and spoke. "I give myself a B-, Ms. Lindy." He began to drum the fingers of his right hand against the wall. "I know I deserve an F. I was on a bike in the weight room, and I saw the doors open and I just sat there, looking. I didn't see how scared Charysse was. I didn't even hear the guys making noise. If it had been me, I know

I would have dropped dead of a heart attack. I couldn't even move, to help her. I just saw this beautiful girl and…froze."

Norm's hands stopped moving. His hips stopped shifting. He seemed to stop breathing as he stared forward, his eyes fixed on something unseen. The class, even Ms. Lindy and Mr. Kennedy, watched in awe as Norm stood perfectly, utterly, miraculously still. But then his left foot shot out, twitching madly and making everyone in the room jump as Norm shuddered out of his reverie and back into his usual self. The rest of his body followed suit and resumed its weight-shifting, toe-tapping, drumming and twitching.

"I've never gotten a grade lower than a B in my life and that was in PE, so it really doesn't count. I busted the curve in Quantum Physics, so the lowest grade I can get and still finish the year with a 4.0 is a B-. I'm sorry, Charysse." He sat down and shrank behind his laptop screen. "But I can't wreck my GPA because of what Mackenzie did to you."

Ms. Lindy wrote a few notes on a piece of paper. "I accept your grade, Norm. Next?"

Candice slowly stood. She was dressed in the brown pants and beige shirt she had been wearing the first day Charysse met her. Her face was free of makeup and her hair hung loose, which made her dark roots much more noticeable. She looked weary and terrified. When she spoke, her words ran together in a strange monotone. "I-I give myself a B," she said, staring at her hands. "Given that we had no idea what we were being graded on for this class, it's not fair to give myself anything less than a passing grade. What happened to Charysse wasn't premeditated and it was just horseplay that got out of hand. I still face disciplinary action from the school. If I gave myself anything less than a passing grade, I'd be punished twice for the same lapse in judgment. I give myself a B."

Ms. Lindy spent a long moment writing notes on a fresh sheet of paper before she looked up at Candice. "Look at me, Candice," she said gently. Candice raised her wan face. "Now tell me what grade you would have given yourself if you hadn't been told what to say."

Candice used the nail of one thumb to tear at the cuticle of the other one. She bowed her head and her hair fell to partially cloak her face.

"Don't you say a word," Mackenzie whispered. "They're just trying to trap you."

"Shut up, Mackenzie," Candice sighed. The exhaled words had the effect of a slap on Mackenzie. Her mouth dropped open and she whipped her head around to look at the girl she had likely wounded more deeply than she had hurt Charysse. "I'd give myself an F," Candice said. "I deserve to flunk this class because I did things that I knew were wrong, just so I could be popular. I wore clothes that I hated, I went to parties that I hated, and I hurt someone that I really like." Candice looked up and tears streamed down her cheeks. "I give myself an F because I let so many bad things happen to Charysse and to myself." She turned to Charysse. "I'm so sorry! I wish I knew why I acted the way I did. It makes me so sick when I think about it all. I'm so, so sorry!"

Whether it was proper or not, Charysse left her desk and went to Candice. She held her, letting her wet her shoulder with her tears. "I'm not mad, okay?" Charysse soothed. "I was never mad at you. I was worried about you. All of us ... me, Shane, Lotus, Marty and Chrysanthemum. We've been waiting for you."

Candice cried a little harder. "Ms. Lindy," Charysse said, "could I take Candice to the bathroom?"

Ms. Lindy's eyes were soft and sympathetic, but her words were hard. "Candice can take herself. Please take your seat, Charysse. Candice, you're excused. And I accept your grade."

"Thank you, Ms. Lindy," Candice sobbed as she left the room.

"If she's not back in two minutes, I'm going after her," Charysse told the teacher. She regretted the warning in her tone, but only so far as it might have disrespected Ms. Lindy and Mr. Kennedy.

Charysse saw that Ms. Lindy shared her concern when the teacher nodded her approval.

"I'll go next," Lotus said. She stood and the strips of black chiffon comprising the skirt of her dress floated about her hips and calves. "I give myself a D," she said firmly. "I underestimated

Mackenzie. Or, I overestimated Charysse." She smiled at Charysse, who answered with one of her own. "I never would have left Charysse alone in the locker room if I'd known what was going to happen."

"How could you know what was going to happen?" Ms. Lindy asked.

"I couldn't. I didn't. But I know Mackenzie. And I know how much she dislikes Charysse. Given those facts, I suppose it was only a matter of time and opportunity before something really bad happened. I give myself a D because instead of assuming that my friend could handle herself when it came to Mackenzie, I should have been there to back her up."

One of the rare Eichorn students who cared as much about grades as she cared about the price of wind on Neptune, Lotus sat down with a smile.

"I accept your grade, Miss Achearn," Ms. Lindy said. "Mr. McKenna, I'd like to hear from you next."

"I'd like to submit an F for my grade," Shane said as he stood.

"Mr. McKenna," Ms. Lindy started. "Shane…you were the only one who went to Charysse's aid. Why do you believe you deserve an F?"

"I stood up for Charysse too late. I should have said something when Mackenzie destroyed her Lemke paper. Instead, I kept quiet and hoped Mackenzie would get over whatever it is that makes her hate Charysse so much." Shane sat back down.

"Thank you, Mr. McKenna," Ms. Lindy said. "I accept your grade."

Charysse stood, smoothing her hands over the legs of her jeans as she did so. She smiled when Candice slipped into the room and went back to her desk. "I deserve an F. I should have stood up for myself a long time ago. I should have told Mackenzie Cole to go to hell, and if that didn't work, I should have reported her to Mr. Kennedy. What happened yesterday was partially my fault because I did nothing to make Mackenzie believe that she couldn't get away with it. I let her bother me all semester, so of course she thought she could do whatever she wanted to me. I deserve an F, but this was a lesson I've learned very well."

"Thank you, Charysse. I accept your grade."

"Can I go next, Ms. Lindy?" Donovan asked. When she nodded, he stood. "I don't really know what to say. I think the human body is a thing of beauty and I honestly don't think Charysse should have been embarrassed. I mean, I can see how she felt. I really can." He faced Charysse. "You didn't have anything to be embarrassed about, Charysse. Mackenzie's the one who looked like a fool, not you."

"Your grade, Donovan?" Ms. Lindy prompted.

"Incomplete?"

"I accept," Ms. Lindy said.

Mackenzie shot to her feet. "First of all, I give myself an A. I played your stupid game, Ms. Lindy. I showed that I'm a domineering, manipulative and forceful person. I'm a born leader and obviously you resent me for it. It was a *prank*. Who knew it would have the effect it did?" Mackenzie opened her arms wide and laughed. "I didn't know that the weight room was full of boys, or that Charysse's towel would come off. And I'm not the one who took her clothes."

"You got Bea to do it," Candice said.

"Prove it," Mackenzie snapped over her shoulder.

"I reject your grade," Ms. Lindy said. "Care to try again?"

Mackenzie took a leisurely step toward Ms. Lindy's desk. "My father told me that the grades in this class don't factor into our GPAs. They don't matter one bit."

"That's true," Ms. Lindy said. "But my comments on your transcripts will matter quite a lot to the admissions officers of the colleges you've applied to, Miss Cole."

"I did some research on you, Ms. Lindy," Mackenzie said. "You may have graduated from Eichorn, but you have a perfect I.Q. Perfectly *normal*. You're average. You went to junior college for two years before you transferred to Brown University. You graduated in three years and got your master's in one. And you wrote a few books. So what? That hardly qualifies you to teach students like us. Maybe we should be grading *you*."

Mr. Kennedy rose from his chair. "Miss Cole, I would have thought that our talk in my office yesterday would have taught you something, but I see now that Ms. Lindy was being kind when she told me that you are brilliant, beautiful and heartless. That you have no conscience, no compassion, and that your brand of genius is a menace to an unsuspecting world."

"She's a complete fraud, yet you're taking her side?" Mackenzie wailed.

"Ms. Lindy's genius is her ability to bring out the very best in others," Mr. Kennedy said sternly. "She has the unique ability to read and assess character and intellect. Police departments across the country have used her to assist with interrogations of some of the most infamous criminals in this country's history. The president invites her to sit in on meetings with foreign heads of state. Every college admissions counselor in North America knows Ms. Lindy's name, and her comments on a transcript can make or break an acceptance. We at Eichorn use her to help shape fine characters for the fine minds that may someday change this world. Ms. Lindy is no fraud, young lady. It's only by her intervention, and that of Charysse DiGregorio, that you didn't find yourself expelled yesterday."

"Wh-What?" Mackenzie sputtered.

"Charysse and I met with Mr. Kennedy this morning before this grading session to discuss suitable punishments for you and your cohorts," Ms. Lindy said. "It was only fair to include Charysse, considering that she was the victim of your actions. I recommended expulsion. Charysse agreed to Mr. Kennedy's recommendation of in-class suspensions, with one condition."

"Which is?" Mackenzie sneered.

"An apology," Charysse said. "That's all I want from you."

"Candice, as you have already apologized to Miss DiGregorio, you will receive a three-day in-class suspension that will be removed from your permanent record in June, if you can keep your nose clean through next semester," Mr. Kennedy said. "Miss Cole, does that arrangement suit you as well?"

Mackenzie seemed to quiver with rage as her eyes bored into Charysse. Two days ago, Charysse would have averted her gaze, turning her attention to one of her friends and pretending that Mackenzie didn't even exist. Things were different now. In some elemental way, Charysse was different now. She was strong enough to stare Mackenzie down, to let her know with a mere look that she was no longer a thing to be humiliated and abused.

"Why do you hate me so much, Mackenzie?" Charysse asked.

"If you're such a genius, you figure it out," Mackenzie snapped.

"I have," Charysse said. "I just want to make sure that you know. Until you do, you won't be able to change. You seem to think that being smart entitles you to something bigger and better than the rest of us. So we can do things that other kids can't. Other kids can do things that we can't. We're all the same, when you get right down to it. Marty's an amazing guy who only wants to be thought of as normal. Candice is a true genius, until she has to face a problem that doesn't come out of a book. Lotus manipulates color and shadow and light beautifully, to create beauty from paper and paint. Shane is the most mature guy I know because he's aware of his weaknesses, his faults and his mistakes. All he wants..." She paused, her eyes meeting Shane's. She had to swallow back a tiny lump before continuing. "All he wants is to know that his best is good enough. Then there's me, the unknown quantity. I've never been tested. I'm the most ordinary creature in this room, and you know what? That's what makes me remarkable.

"You refuse to see what your problem is, Mackenzie, so I'm going to do you a favor and tell you. You think normal is a disadvantage. You manipulate people. You zero in on weakness, and you prey on it. No one in this room is better than anyone else in it or outside of it. Why can't you realize that?"

Charysse was aware of the eyes of the room on her. She and Mackenzie both had the genius of Intuition, and they both knew what the outcome of Mackenzie's inner battle would be. So Charysse wasn't surprised when Mackenzie swung her hate-filled gaze to Ms. Lindy and Mr. Kennedy and said, "You can stuff your apology."

The headmaster sighed heavily. "Then you're out, Miss Cole."

Mackenzie snatched up her backpack and stomped out of the room.

"Shall we continue?" Ms. Lindy asked as if nothing unusual had happened. "Chrysanthemum?"

Charysse barely heard a word Chrysanthemum said as she gave herself a C, and explained her reasons for grading herself so. Even though she knew it wasn't her fault, she couldn't believe that Mackenzie would rather get expelled in the middle of her senior year, rather than utter a simple apology. Charysse felt more and more ill as the grading session stretched on, seemingly without end.

*

"I can't believe Ms. Lindy rejected your C and gave you an A," Lotus said to Marty as they walked with Charysse to the Arts & Music Hall, where the three hoped to find their finals grades posted outside their Music Appreciation class. "I'm still trying to figure out why she did it."

"I don't know," Marty said. "Ms. Lindy works in mysterious ways."

"She did it because you're the only one who stood up to Mackenzie all along," Charysse explained quietly. "I still can't believe that Mackenzie let herself be expelled yesterday. She should have just apologized. Or she could have accepted the school's offer to get her counseling, like Candice did. It's so scary to think that she would throw her whole Eichorn career away out of hatred for me. Do you think Mackenzie's spot will be filled for next semester?"

"Who knows?" Marty said. "It would be weird having some kid come in just for half a year."

"Have Bea and Leslie apologized to you yet?" Lotus asked. Marty pulled open the glass door of the Arts & Music Hall and held it open for the two girls. Two boys were leaving the building. They turned and craned their necks to stare at Charysse as they skipped down the short flight of stairs in front of the entrance.

"Haven't you guys ever seen a naked body before?" Marty yelled. "What, you don't have cable?"

Charysse bit her lower lip. Even though the Locker Room Incident was over, as far as she was concerned, boys and girls alike continued to stare at her. Even one of the male coaches seemed to look at her oddly now. This was the last day of school before break, and it was only third period. She prayed that she could get through the day without dying of embarrassment.

"I'll catch you guys at lunch," Charysse said. She hurried up the wide stairwell to the second floor before Lotus and Marty could question her about ditching them. She knew that Marty was only trying to help by verbally attacking anyone who gave Charysse so much as a sideways glance, but all his actions did was draw more attention to her.

Bea and Leslie had been waiting at Charysse's locker for her when she arrived at school. They had apologized for the locker room, for Lemke's paper and for things Charysse had never known that they'd done. They made Charysse feel as though she had rescued them from a POW camp rather than simply getting Mackenzie expelled.

"But I didn't get Mackenzie expelled…did I?" Charysse dragged her feet as she moved to the giant, semi-circular window on the landing between the first and second floors. The windowsill was cushioned so students could practice music or draw or study while enjoying the view of Eichorn's man-made lake on one side, and a two-story peek into the painting arena on the other side. The window had become one of her favorite spots, along with the grape arbor in the greenhouse.

Charysse sat on the windowsill. She hugged her knees to her chest and leaned against the window. Her breath made a foggy patch on the cold glass. The lake was frozen and covered with snow. The trees surrounding it stuck their bare, crooked black branches into the pale gray sky. The view before her was as bare and lonely and disconsolate as she suddenly felt. When her tears started, she made no effort to stop or hide them.

She had been weeping for a good few minutes before she noticed Shane sitting at her feet. "Hi," she sniffled into the sleeve of her cable-knit sweater.

"Hi," he responded.

"Everything sort of caught up to me just now." She tried to smile through her tears, but her mouth only managed a pained grimace. "I feel so bad for Mackenzie."

"Why?" She grunted in bewilderment. "After everything she said and did to you, why are you crying for her?"

"It makes me sad that everyone, even her so-called friends, is happy to see her gone. My dad used to tell me to always find the good in people, and I tried to find it in Mackenzie, but I couldn't. That makes me sad, too. To know that she's so damaged."

"You said that you knew why she hated you. Why did she, Charysse?"

"Because we're so much alike."

"You and Mackenzie?" he laughed.

"We're both good at reading people. We're both overachievers. We had the same interest in you. I think she thought that by coming to Eichorn, I was taking something from her."

"That was her problem," Shane said. "Not yours."

"I didn't even try to be friends with her, Shane, and I should have. Even if she stung me twice as hard, I should have tried." Charysse sobbed miserably as she acknowledged her own failing. "I don't believe that she's this horrible, naturally evil person. She hurt me because she must be in a lot of pain herself. Now we're both suffering."

"I never thought of it like that before, from Mackenzie's side," he said. "I've gone to school with her my whole life, and I know her parents put a lot of pressure on her to be the best. I remember once, when we were in the third grade, we were pilgrims in the Thanksgiving pageant. Mackenzie and I had to recite these huge speeches. I got through mine just fine. Memorizing five pages wasn't a big deal for me. But Mackenzie forgot the last part of hers. I'd memorized hers, too, just because I'd heard it so many times in practice.

"After the show, her mom and dad cornered her backstage and called her lazy, careless, incompetent and a disgrace. It was harsh, and all over some stupid line. One of the teachers had to ask them to stop. Mackenzie was only nine. If her parents act that way in public, I can only imagine how they treat her at home."

"I hope she'll be okay," Charysse whispered.

"Will you be okay?"

"This is really hard," she admitted. "I agree with Donovan, that it was just skin people saw. But it was *my* skin!" Her chin trembled with a new rush of tears. "I wish I could be more mature about the whole thing and just get over it."

Shane held her and stroked her back, smoothing her hair. "It'll get better. Just as soon as the yahoos find something else to talk about."

Charysse turned toward the painting arena to blow her nose. Lotus was in there with Marty. He was laughing as Lotus tossed paint at a wall-sized canvas, her latest work for a German banking firm. "Marty got an A from Ms. Lindy," Charysse said. "He's the only one. Some good came from my strip act after all."

"You know how something will happen, and years later you look back on it and realize how wonderful that moment was? You didn't appreciate it when it happened, but in retrospect, you know it was one of the greatest things to ever happen to you."

Charysse smiled through her tears. "If you're about to tell me that what happened Monday will someday be one of my greatest memories…I'll have to strongly disagree. Everyone keeps staring at me. I find myself checking to make sure I actually have clothes on."

"I'm not talking about you." He switched places with her and positioned her to lay her head on his shoulder. "I'm talking about me. And right now." He tilted her face toward his. His eyes moved over her features as though he were trying to program each curve and freckle, and each angle and shadow into a special place in his memory.

The sweet and somber tones of a cello in the practice rooms below wafted up to their ears. Charysse's eyes felt raw and scratchy from crying, and she knew she looked a fright as Shane caressed her face with his tender gaze. His fingertip tickled along her jaw line. He stared into her eyes as he said, "I'll remember this forever."

"You'll remember how red and puffy my eyes get when I cry?"

"I'll remember how strong you are, and how much you had to take before anyone could make you cry," he corrected.

*

"I am *not* walking in with you, dude," came Marty's muffled voice from the other side of the emergency exit next to the Transfers table.

Charysse and Lotus looked at each other curiously. Marty opened the door just enough to squeeze through. He sat down at the table, pulled his micro-point permanent pen from his pocket, and began covering the last few square inches of the Transfers table with the maze he'd begun in September.

Charysse pushed her lunch, homemade stuffed shells and a garden salad, over to Marty. He looked at Chrysanthemum, who lifted her eyes from her book long enough to give Marty a look that told him that Charysse still wasn't quite herself. "Share this with me, Char," Marty said, adopting Bonnie's nickname for her.

"I'm not hungry," Charysse insisted. "It's hard to eat with a hundred people staring at you."

"No one's star—" Marty started. But then he looked around and saw that people actually were staring at the Transfers table, and more specifically at Charysse. Marty stood to yell at all of them when the emergency exit behind him opened. Shane walked in, and for the first time all semester, Chrysanthemum pulled her face completely out of her book.

Lotus turned around to see what had made her twin's eyes turn into two wide orbs of crystalline blue. Her own eyes nearly popped from her skull when she caught sight of Shane. Lotus grabbed Charysse's arm hard enough to leave finger marks.

Charysse looked up. "Shane's gone Jamie," Charysse muttered, her face paralyzed in shock.

Shane stood at the Transfers table for a moment, smiling as he waved at his friends. All eyes followed him as he strolled through the cafeteria to the end of the food line. Wearing a dazzling white smile and a pair of equally bright tube socks—and nothing else—Shane grabbed a tray and took a place in line. He asked for his meal choice twice before the server stopped looking at him long enough to pick up a pair of tongs and place food on his plate.

Conversations had ceased upon Shane's entrance. By the time he was at the cash register station paying for his lunch—with a five-dollar bill he pulled from his right sock—students were clapping and whistling. Donovan and a few other boys had taken off their shirts and were whirling them over their heads.

Shane started back to the Transfers table, pausing to nod a greeting to a table full of stunned teachers. Ms. Lindy's face was the only one that remained completely unreadable. At the Transfers table, Shane set down his tray and pulled out a chair. "Could you hold my change for me?" he asked Charysse. "No pockets." He patted the place on his bare backside where his pockets ordinarily would have been.

Charysse, who had yet to blink, offered her palm and accepted the loose change. Shane sat down. The cold metal edging surrounding the padded center of the chair made him sing a note of surprise.

Marty hunkered lower over his maze. "Did you really have to get the corndog instead of the soup?"

"I'm not dressed for hot soup," Shane said. "I forgot mustard." He started to get up.

"I'll get it!" the twins cried in unison. Lotus, in her Empire-style blouse, and Chrysanthemum, in her overalls, scurried off.

"Marty, could you pass me one of those mustard packets?" Shane asked, nodding toward the mustard someone had left behind on a nearby table.

"Dude, I am totally not touching you," Marty chuckled. "It's all I can do to sit at the same table with you."

"You had clothes on when I saw you during third period," Charysse said, a bemused smile of astonishment brightening her face. "What happened since then?"

"I decided to dress for lunch," he said. "Or undress." He crossed his arms on the table and leaned toward her.

Charysse was impressed by his casual demeanor. But then she was blushing enough for both of them. "I like your socks."

"I'm not as brave as you are. I didn't have the guts to go buck."

"Why are you doing this?" she whispered urgently.

"Because I wanted to give all of them something else to talk about and stare at." He looked into her eyes and Charysse saw the naked honesty in them. "And because I love you."

His humble, heartfelt admission left her speechless. All she could do was throw her arms around him.

"Mr. McKenna, may I loan you my coat?" Mr. Kennedy stood behind Shane, holding out his blazer.

"No, but thank you, Mr. Kennedy," Shane said as Charysse reluctantly released him. "It's actually pretty warm in here. Thank goodness, or I'd really be embarrassed right about now."

"Mr. McKenna, trust me," Mr. Kennedy said. "You'll want this when you're crossing the campus to come to my office."

"That's my cue, guys," Shane said. Mr. Kennedy set the jacket over Shane's shoulders, so he was covered—mostly—when he stood. "I'll see you guys after school."

"I, for one, hope to see less of you," Marty said.

To the applause of his schoolmates, Shane followed Mr. Kennedy toward the headmaster's office. When Shane again passed Ms. Lindy, she stopped him. "Shane," she said, "that grade of yours that doesn't count in my class? It just became an A+."

*

Charysse was sitting in the senior lounge only half listening to the conversation of the group of girls surrounding her. She kept her eyes on the window. The silent lullaby of the fresh snow falling would have made her sleepy if she hadn't been watching to see Shane exit the headmaster's office at the rear of the main building. All of Eichorn's seniors—with the exception of Mackenzie and Shane—were gathered in the lounge for their class Holiday party. Bradley and a group of other boys played the Dreidl game for real money instead of Hanukkah gelt, and Marty was having a Silly String fight with Donovan, Candice, the Achearn twins and about ten other students.

The second she saw a fully-dressed Shane leaving the main building, Charysse grabbed her wool coat. She put it on as she ran outside. She met him on the cement path halfway between the main building and Corcoran Hall. "Did he kill you?" she asked.

"Yes, but it wasn't so bad." Shane took Charysse's hand and led her away from both buildings, to the untrodden snow in the grove of evergreens between the library and the science and technology building. "He gave me a speech about decency and impulsiveness, he called my parents and told me to write a fifty-page paper on social mores and public nudity."

"Wow," Charysse mumbled. "I suppose it could have been worse."

"Yeah, I suppose."

"You could have been kicked out of school. You risked a lot for me." Charysse stopped. "Thank you. But don't ever do anything like that again."

"Do you want to stay here for the senior class party, or would you rather cut out early?" he asked. "We could hang out at my house before the limo arrives for our Lindy dinner."

"I kind of wanted to stay here a little longer," she admitted. "Everyone seems to have forgotten about my Lady Godiva routine." She grinned. "They're all being so nice to me now."

Shane raised his head toward the sky and let the new fall of snow dust his face. It made lacy patterns in his hair and on his clothes, and in that moment, Charysse wished that she had Lotus's genius, or Chrysanthemum's, so she could preserve Shane's beauty in pictures or words.

"Shane?"

"Hmm?"

"Did I look ridiculous in the weight room?"

Shane gripped her upper arms. His breath mingled with hers in the snowy air as he slowly shook his head. The gentle and adoring way he looked at her told her that she hadn't looked ridiculous to him. Not at all.

The unspoken compliment sent a very pleasant rush of heat to Charysse's face, planting roses in her cheeks. She stopped and scooped up handfuls of snow and packed them into a loose snowball. She tossed it at Shane and it exploded against his chest. She turned and ran deeper into the grove with Shane's footfalls crunching after her. He stopped to collect some snow and tossed it at her. They chased each other, pelting each other with snow until they were breathless and the tips of their noses were tinged with pink. Charysse's joyous laughter echoed through the evergreens.

"I've never heard you laugh like this before," Shane panted as he caught her by her hand. "It's like music."

She started to run away again but Shane pulled her in close. He slid his right arm around her waist and cupped her face with his left hand. His eyes kissed her lips for the longest time before he bowed his head and touched his lips to hers.

If it was still cold, Charysse didn't notice. If Eichorn collapsed into rubble, Charysse wouldn't have cared. She was aware of Shane's warmth as he held her, and the soft sigh he uttered when she put her arms around him. She didn't breathe, she didn't think, she couldn't even move as Shane's lips warmed hers. When cool air replaced them, it took her a moment to open her eyes.

"Was that okay?" he asked, still holding her. "I should have asked before I did that."

"It was nice," Charysse said dreamily. "It was wonderful."

"I think we should practice more over break," Shane decided.

Charysse laughed and started toward Corcoran Hall. "What are you wearing to Polcari's tonight?"

"I don't know." He kissed her mittened hand. "Is it formal?"

"I don't think so."

"Good," Shane grinned, "because I don't think I have any black socks."

Crystal Hubbard is an award-winning author as well as a former reporter and Boston Herald sports copy editor. A native of Missouri, she attended the St. Louis Public School System's Gifted Program. She spent most of her life on the East coast, primarily in Boston and Eastern Massachusetts. She is a mother of four and she writes full time. Her hobbies include reading, writing, cooking, sewing, boxing, watching television, and wrestling with advanced geometry problems, although she does not like math. She is an avid Red Sox fan. Her previous young adult novels include *Alive and Unharmed*, and *Million Dollar Girl*, written under the pen name of Anne Wilde. Please visit Crystal Hubbard Books on Facebook to learn more about the author and her work.

Made in the USA
Charleston, SC
30 December 2013